BE SAFE

DOUG WEAVER

BLACK❦ROSE
writing™

ISBN: 978-1-61296-808-7
PUBLISHED BY BLACK ROSE WRITING
www.blackrosewriting.com

Printed in the United States of America
Suggested retail price $17.95

Be Safe is printed in Book Antiqua
Cover art courtesy of Richard Frost

Special thanks to Katharine Haake

Dedicated to the memory of George James, whose humor, wit and intelligence continue to inspire.

BE SAFE

CHAPTER ONE

Maybe I should try to be still for a minute – just sit my ass down on one of these long wooden benches lining this cavernous hallway inside the Criminal Courts Building over on Temple. But I'm nervous – scared actually, so I'm walking back and forth trying to look casual amid all these hundreds of gang members and lowlifes, many of whom, despite finding themselves in such a forbidding setting, have tried to dress in a way that bridges the criminal/citizen divide. They've abandoned baggy shorts and tank tops in favor of too large dark plaid shirts and tan khakis that they believe engender both servility to The System: *Yes, your Honor;* and threats to Everybody Else: *You lookin' at me, bitch*? There are tons of lawyers too, who are waiting for their clients to show up, as well as what appear to be truly saddened and befuddled family members of the recently arrested. And the DA – or I guess not *the* DA, but one of his assistants because I'm not like involved with Charles Manson or anything – I'm just a guy suffering a mid-life crisis of sorts – and not like a regular run-of-the-mill mid-life crisis because those are pretty much codified as bouts of unregulated spending on stuff like sports cars or other non-age appropriate vehicles, which, to me, isn't really a crisis, but whatever.

Anyway, I'm pacing this hallway and this Assistant DA calls my name: "Albert Sykes?" And there's a question mark at the end because he's putting a tired-sounding query out into the air because he doesn't know what I look like. We've never met and he's subpoenaed me to be a witness in this theft case. My truck was stolen and I'm supposed to testify for the prosecution – for this Assistant DA. And this is kind of ironic because my mid-life crisis is different than most. I'm like this middle-aged guy with a slight drug habit who's always having sex, like you'd think I'm trying to wear out my dick, trying to have so much sex that I eventually become asexual like a sloe-eyed steer who's burned through his allotted number of lifetime ejaculations so he can spend his golden years munching cud while not being particularly bothered by memories of how vibrant life used to be before his organ went permanently limp, or, god forbid, before he developed a prolapsed asshole, which is a condition – *I've heard* – that isn't that uncommon among certain members of society. I'm also a dealer of methamphetamine, so you'd think I'd be on the other side of the scales of justice thing. But my truck really was stolen during a midday sex party by a couple of strangers from Central America. Meth makes me feel really fucking horny, as well as it's a drug that fits me better than heroin, because that was actually the drug I started with. But the thing about heroin use – especially overdoses – is that you're not really awake to enjoy the experience, unless being really fucking sleepy is your vision of moonlight, but whatever. All I remember about this time I used heroin is this girl with long red hair – Betsy Ross – no shit – that was literally her name – gave me a shot of dope in my armpit. She'd been a registered nurse at one point in her life, so I was assured by her boyfriend, this bisexual guy named Duffy, that she knew what she was doing so there was no risk, and it would hit me faster than it otherwise would if a vein in my arm had been used. Her hair kept falling in front of her eyes, so she was constantly shaking her head so she could see better as she probed the flesh of my armpit with her delicate fingers before plunging the needle in. Apparently armpit veins are surrounded with essential nerves and other important biological stuff, which non-nurse folks might not know about. And I didn't know about Duffy's sexuality firsthand, meaning that I never had sex with him. I didn't, not because I didn't like guys. I'm 100 percent queer – "queer" in this case meaning homosexual – not some vague academically-inclined "other" clutching to some theoretical category of rebel/outcast while brandishing a theoretical middle finger to some real or theoretical status quo. And I'm not saying that academics are wrong – it's just obvious to me that dope fiends are the real queers if you think about it. Dope fiends – homo or hetero or whatever – I'm laughing right now thinking about it – even the most normal acting dope fiends – I'll talk about meth addicts, because, you know, that's my thing – I'm trying to imagine what a shit storm a meth addict's baby shower would turn out to be. Addicts may allow themselves a grand total of maybe twenty-five minutes of ennoblement for the realm of baby-dom – certainly not enough time to become gainfully employed so they can buy baby formula and baby clothes – and – I can hardly breathe the word – *nurture* – a newborn human being so he or she can fit into some preplanned societal arc that includes Stanford or UCLA – or even Mordor, just for variety's sake. But the meth addict, it would take maybe three seconds before a newborn will become just another ass-brained art project where Daddy or Mommy will smear little four-week old Amanda with white glue and then roll her in glitter just because it looks pretty. So I guess I'm an authentic queer: I shoot dope *and* I suck cock.

It's just that Duffy wasn't really my cup of tea. He looked like a six-foot-three vampire with powder white skin and he had this enormous red mouth that, no matter what expression he was emoting, his lips and mouth always seemed to look like they were artificial, kind of like they'd been painted onto his face. I never even fantasized about the size of his cock, which guys pretty much just assume that they're huge on guys as tall as Duffy. I just wanted to learn every bit of drug lore he had, so I guess I strung him along. I'm pretty good at cock teasing, so we went along like that for months and months, me getting high for free and him getting frustrated as anything. But this night I used heroin, all I really remember is the needle going in – there was this great ritual quality to the whole thing. Duffy and Betsy had lit all these candles and they wore these Asian sort of slinky silk robes they'd stolen from one of the costume houses in Hollywood – there're millions of them in all these different little garages in alleys off Fountain Avenue. And Betsy had me lie flat on my back and raise my arms above my head, and then she swabbed my armpit with alcohol, which to this day, even at the doctor's office, every time I smell alcohol being swabbed before I get a shot or have blood drawn, I get this memory of that night way back then. But all I remember about using this heroin is waking up – or coming to, really, and I was all constrained inside a pretty small sleeping bag – only my head was sticking out. But I woke up and I felt really good, like I'd just had this great night's sleep, and I couldn't understand why I was inside this sleeping bag. "What's going on," I said, which kind of startled Betsy and Duffy. And she came over and said something like, "Man, you're *really* lucky," and Duffy concurred. They said they thought I died – overdosed – because I turned blue and they couldn't tell if I was breathing or not, so they zipped me up into this sleeping bag so they could wait until it got late enough so they could take me over to Echo Park and dump me into the middle of this huge lotus patch on one end of the lake there, which I've since come to learn was a pretty common method for disposing of unwanted corpses, which sort of makes you wonder about corpses of the wanted variety. Anyway, that was when there were actually lotuses in the lake. People used to travel from all over the world to see these lotuses because it was supposedly the biggest lotus patch in the northern hemisphere. The City of Los Angeles actually put together a lotus festival in Echo Park every August ostensibly to celebrate the beauty of these lotuses and the size of the lotus patch, but really it was just an excuse to make a few bucks off selling burritos and tamales. And really, the lotuses were pretty magnificent. They're these really beautiful gigantic blossoms that kind of float in the shallows and they're surrounded by these huge dark green leaves that form pretty much an unbroken membrane over the surface of the water. And it was these huge leaves that made Echo Park Lake so attractive for dumping bodies, because you could throw anything into the lotus patch, and these leaves would immediately give way and part, swallowing up whatever it was you threw in there – something small like a bowling ball or big like a body – and then they'd snap right back into place like nothing at all had happened. It was perfect for a couple of reasons: First, Echo Park Lake was a lot closer than having to drive all the way to Griffith Park, which was the traditional dumping ground for dead bodies – and Second, you didn't really even need a car. A lot of local folks just used shopping carts to wheel the recently deceased over to the lake late at night. And after they dumped their bodies, instead of returning the shopping carts to where they found them, they would just leave them there around the lake because the local supermarkets would drive around every morning and collect them. But then some Parks and Recreation employees, in the process of discharging their parks and recreation maintenance duties, had waded into this lotus patch one morning and discovered a dead body, which caused the wheels of government to shift into high gear, and they called in these earth moving tractors that really tore the shit out of this lotus patch looking for more bodies, and they found about twelve of them. Anyway, since then, the lotus patch is just this tiny single lotus plant all alone at one end of this lake. Sad. They're trying to grow them back, but not having much success. It makes you wonder if it was the bodies that provided the nourishment that made the lotus patch so successful in the first place. But the Lotus Festival still goes on every August, but it's not the same as when there were actually lotuses there to celebrate.

So after I walk up and introduce myself to this Assistant DA, I explain to him that I really hate the name Albert, that I go by Bert now, even though I'm not in love with that name either, but it's better than Al, which, to me seems pretty red-necked; that I would have preferred to have a cooler name like Shane or Curtis instead of Al-Bert, because that's such a clunky name. I sense there's a certain level of skepticism in the ether surrounding him and his minions, like they're not exactly sure how I'm going to come off on the witness stand because it's pretty obvious that my mind wanders sometimes. And my value as a believable witness is shrinking right before their eyes. "Tell me what happened," the lawyer says.

So I let loose. I don't try to varnish anything. I just say that these guys who stole my truck had showed up with a friend of mine who was visiting me because I was trying to put together this crazy sex party in the middle of the day. And these two guys were visiting from El Salvador or something – anyway, they weren't exactly 100 percent gay, which made the whole scenario just that much more exciting – to me, not the Assistant DA, but who knows. I mean there's these two dudes who only speak a couple of words of English – and they've got a bit more fat on them than I'm used to, but whatever. Once they started getting high on meth, the clothes flew off and everybody jumped into the bed like a bunch of horny monkeys.

And one of these legal minions pipes up and says: "HIV positive or negative?"

And this creates an immediate dilemma. If I say negative, I'm thinking it won't be too difficult to find out that I'm positive, even though I'm not sure that checking some Health Department database is something they'd even do, but if they did, my declaration might be used to show a certain level of deviousness, which could, right away, be placed into the prosecution's quiver of legal strategies known as "an act in furtherance," which locates any fucking behavior at all – blowing your nose, ordering a burrito, nodding your head – into the realm of intent. So I answer truthfully: "Positive. HIV positive."

And this admission puts the brakes on the whole line of questioning, because the Assistant DA and minions kind of get together and whisper for a bit. And then the lawyer just straight up asks me: "Do you want to acquire legal counsel before we continue?"

And I know exactly where this is headed, because I didn't mention any kind of forewarning to my what's assumed to be HIV negative sex partners from Central America, even though they're the ones who stole my truck, so you'd think, because of my standing as a victim, I might be entitled to at least a little bit of slack, but whatever. So right away my brain starts some unplanned-for heavy lifting, testing theories and their plausibility quotients. I could say I just don't remember if I told them I had HIV or not, but that gets the nix right away because I'm not a complete idiot. I've seen tons and tons of cop shows, and not remembering never amounts to anything. I could say I just assumed the guy these thieves showed up with – my "friend," that it was common knowledge around town that he had AIDS, so I just figured that he spilled the beans. And me being a pretty efficient guy, I didn't feel like needlessly repeating this information, which actually may or may not be what I was thinking at the time. I honestly don't remember. And the lawyer can see he knows what I'm thinking, because he just says, "Yeah, you could be charged with attempted murder." But he doesn't want to get into this at all because all I have to say is that I didn't *actually* have sexual contact with these guys; I was more of a spectator; that I just sat on the sidelines and watched all this crazy sex, which to me seemed more twisted and weird than if I participated. And he seemed totally relieved by this admission and says that he'll call me on the day that I'll be needed to testify at this guy's preliminary hearing. He doesn't extend his hand or anything, just nods his head and says good-bye.

CHAPTER TWO

Gallagher, a forty-three-year-old recent graduate of Cri-Life Recovery House, complains to Rogarth, thirty-seven, who was recently booted from same recovery house for harboring improper intentions regarding sobriety, sex, god and community – a revelation divined by Rick something-or-other (the one with the teeth), Rogarth's CDW, an initialism derived from the title, Chemical Dependency Worker, a somewhat ennobled label that grew from the amazingly well-attended courses in the field of Drug and Alcohol Counseling, a curriculum at virtually every two-year college in the state, and a label that used to be simply "counselor." Drug and Alcohol Counseling classes fill up fast, as greater numbers of people suffer drug convictions, which banishes them to trudge increasingly steep and ever more narrowing avenues toward career building that are available to second-class citizens, and as a result, every new semester these classes take up more and more space in class catalogues. And why not? Why not elevate what's widely believed to be a stain on the human condition to the status of academic discipline? Why not permit – actually encourage overwhelmed and overpaid administrators who gladly overlook any meaningful context on which to ground their enthusiasm when confronting the never-ending tide of recently-arrested drug-addled neophytes – why not urge these functionaries to allow academic newcomers to study something that they actually seem to be pretty good at, even though it's painfully obvious that any objective evaluation of this strategy will reveal that's it's supported almost 200 percent on both the reality that this course of study is merely an acknowledgement of the impoverished state of the post-academic job market that's available to ex-cons; as well as the unstated and unrealized petty nastiness of insisting that all those who stop using drugs should and must replace any joy afforded by being high with the regimented existence of former addicts who spend most of their waking hours barking to themselves and others that their worst day sober is better than their best day getting high, a proclamation that's just so much bullshit when you think about it, because – well, it's obvious: If getting high were that fucking bad, why have we insisted on doing it for the better part of twenty plus years? Why not take up a legal hobby, like keeping bees or crocheting? But *something's* got to be done with them, right? Because just continuing to lock them up seems like it's counterproductive.

Gallagher tells Rogarth that he's disappointed with his English teacher at Los Angeles City College because he suspects he's a philistine. And even though Rogarth has heard the word "philistine" before, he's not sure what the word means, so he nods his head and listens with fake interest, hoping that Gallagher will spill the definitional beans. But as it turns out, neither of them knows the meaning of the word, so they're stuck nodding their heads to each other, both privately accepting the truth that no truth will be forthcoming, at least about the meaning of this certain word, from this conversation. The men are basically killing time after class, lounging and smoking cigarettes on the mangy lawn that forms what is generously called "the quad" between the school's library and Tinkerton Hall (abbreviated on computer-generated student schedules simply and adorably as Tink, suggesting that any class taught there would be governed by the same rules that administer life in Never Never Land), which might cause one to assume that the building was the home of the drama department, but instead houses most of the college's algebra and English classes, before they have to show up a couple hours early to set up about four hundred folding chairs at what's billed as Los Angeles' biggest All Gay AA Meeting (it's been claimed that it's the biggest All Gay AA Meeting in the universe). One or both of these guys wants more than anything to use the word philistine to the assembled horde of sober homosexuals, if not at this particular venue, then some other sober gathering. But it's Gallagher who'll probably use it – just as he did while talking to Rogarth – to prove to everybody that there's more to him than the overtly spelled out virtues of maintaining a life free from self-induced unconsciousness. Gallagher has heard the word uttered twice.

The second time it was Ryan, who is Gallagher's retirement age AA sponsor, who's had a considerable amount of plastic surgery performed on his face and who injects anabolic steroids into his body, two things that have left him perpetually smiling and muscle bound, and who, in decades past had earned advanced degrees in music – singing to be exact, with a specialization in the art songs of Franz Schubert. His graduation from a Master of Music mill in the Midwest was postponed because his rendition of "Erlkönig," a dramatic song about a dead kid, was less than stellar given the fact that his vocal cords, during a couple of crucial performances, were muddled with phlegm, which he blamed on smoking cocaine. Ryan had said the word in close enough proximity for Gallagher to hear it when describing *Die Kindertotenlieder,* Mahler's series of songs about a shitload of dead kids as sung by Ryan's collegiate archenemy, Debbi Lott, a plump, indelicate, slutty contralto who played softball and believed in Jesus, and whose musical acumen found her sprinting toward and finally pouncing on this or that defenseless leading tone, usually understood to be the essential musical entities that serve as invitations to either end a current phrase or pivot to a new key, a novel approach that more than a couple of operatic dowagers believe led to the creation of the rare yet certainly extant musical direction in *urtext* editions of this or that score, the words *piano pesante*, to a couple of much younger men who admired inflated albeit mature muscles and whose accumulated sober time, unlike Ryan's, who measures his unsullied breathing in decades worth of sober anniversaries, needed to be measured in single-digit months.

Ryan had referred to Miss Lott as a philistine, and he did it in a way that made you think the word smelled bad, like it was a nasty label someone spits out, like "pedophile" or "murderer" or something, but not with as much baggage – and Gallagher, who's not an idiot or anything, figured out right away that "philistine" was a different kind of label; that unlike "pedophile," which everybody knows is fucking little kids, "philistine" probably has more to do with quality or style rather than violating a moral code. But the very first time Gallagher heard "philistine" was when he was still drinking booze and using drugs, mostly meth. Every few months in a seedy part of town made up of dingy storefronts and dirty stucco apartment buildings, down past the 10 Freeway around Washington Boulevard, some industrious guys, who believed they might make a buck or two by exploiting the human penchant for sexual humiliation and degradation, rented a cavernous hall once a month or so in order to hold a surprisingly well-attended gathering that came to be known as The Urine Festival, where men would pay ten or fifteen bucks to come inside, either remove or change their clothes, and piss on each other for a few hours, all the while throwing back as many cans of beer as possible, snorting meth and sniffing poppers. The second or third time Gallagher found himself inside The Urine Festival, there was a group of ten or so guys standing around pissing on a hairless Rubenesque man of about forty who was splayed out inside a bathtub. Since urination held the status of *chef d'oeuvre* at this gathering, there was surprisingly little conversation among the celebrants, something that would have sullied the sullying, and which made it easy to hear the Master of Ceremonies, an obese man with a deep yet mostly effeminate voice, in black leather pants, motorcycle/military cap and Lycra body shirt, who stood on a raised platform and droned quietly into an amplified speaker system, over and over, the words "piss on that fucker...yeah, piss on that fucker." With some amount of effort, Gallagher pushed his way through the small crowd to get a better glimpse of the pissee, and found himself standing next to two men, one dressed in a too-small, faux LAPD uniform, and the other dressed in *Brokeback Mountain* denim and boots, while both vaguely aiming their penises inside the tub, shot robust streams of piss onto the tub dweller while carrying on a clipped sounding, *sotto voce* yet easily discernible conversation about a comparison of the work of David Hockney, especially his early years, when he was disposed to painting swimming pools, both as canvas and subject; and Monet, who painted damp flowers in France. It was during this dialogue that Gallagher first heard the word "philistine." And even though Gallagher wasn't quite sure to which artist this epithet was aimed, he was so impressed by its pejorative potency that it prompted him to mentally bookmark the word for future use, even though he never bothered to look it up in a dictionary.

Regardless, Gallagher has always envied AA speakers who

peppered esoteric words throughout their inspirational speeches. AA is, after all, a program of attraction, so he aspires to use such words, especially into the microphone that's set up at the AA lectern on a stage before hundreds of his peers, most of whom have certain expectations, especially to be dazzled and entertained by whoever's speaking into the P.A. system: *Hello everybody...my name's Gallagher and I'm an addict and an alcoholic. And before I get too far into my spiel here, I want to say that I before I got to these rooms, I was beset with roving hordes of philistines on a daily basis. They're everywhere it seems.* The sad truth is, however, if Gallagher is able to remain in AA for any length of time, he'll realize that it doesn't matter if one uses esoteric words or even English words. No one's going to listen anyway.

All this is predicated, though, on a hard and fast rule in AA: addressing the group as leader, which requires merely introducing yourself and then reading the meeting's format (which is almost always composed by a philistine whose grasp of the rules of syntax and grammar remain realms as unknowable as advanced quantum physics and Aramaic) to the attendees, and especially speaking to the group, which consists of revealing the miraculous route taken from addiction to recovery, credit for which must be given – one more time – to God the Merciful and Most Powerful, and who, it seems, favors this or that speaker over just about everybody else on earth, are great privileges bestowed weekly from The Secretary, whose choices are born not from any sort of flawed motivations shaped by mere appetite and prejudice, but from the lofty realm of principle. Just as the Pope chooses bishops and cardinals, AA secretaries, protected with the shroud of infallibility, choose the leaders and speakers for their meetings from some imagined store of evolved consciousness. So it must be simply a happy coincidence that ninety-eight percent of the leaders and speakers who stand at the lectern before the hundreds of homos at The Wednesday Night Beginners meeting where Rogarth and Gallagher set up the chairs are youthful specimens who could easily have wandered in off the pages of an Abercrombie and Fitch catalogue.

It's said that alcoholism is a disease of perception, which may be a concept yet to be internalized by Gallagher, who isn't exactly A&F material, not because he's a homely or unhandsome man. It's simply because he's a little long in the tooth to be photographed wearing scanty underwear. There have been about forty-nine days in Gallagher's entire life that, when seen through certain gauzy filters, his image could have been chosen to grace the pages of a Sears Catalogue, but they've since been drying up and blowing away at a rate that has placed them, like the California Condor, on an endangered species list, a state of affairs not lost on The Secretary, Sally Boo, sixty something, a perpetually aspiring white-haired cross dresser who somehow maintains an emaciated mien (and is referred to by many of her critics as "that old boiler hen") despite her almost exclusive diet of beef tacos, lemon cake, Oreo cookies and Haagen-Dasz, who'd come to the conclusion within five minutes of meeting Gallagher that his public exposure would be limited to a monthly round of applause for his unselfish service of setting up chairs.

This class of AA service to which Gallagher and Rogarth belong, when viewed objectively through a sociological lens, is of the troglodyte variety: hard-working gay men and some lesbians who, by virtue of their meager physical gifts, remain consigned to an existence of the candle-lighting, coffee making, cookie-replenishing, trash-emptying, water-carrying, stain-mopping level of meeting responsibilities.

On their two-block walk to the corner where they'll stop and purchase a couple of burritos before trekking for another few blocks to the Protestant church where the meeting is held, Rogarth and Gallagher check out a couple of handsome and quite scandalous looking men, an admittedly indefinite descriptor, but one that becomes accurate given the fact that R&G pegged them right away either as guys fresh out of jail or on the verge of getting busted. Out in the daylight walking down the sidewalk, amid the bustle and the commerce and the population, these guys just looked out of place somehow, not unlike American businessmen visiting Riyadh, Saudi Arabia on business trips, who stick out because they've been trained to walk from point A to point B with a practiced resolve, a trait honed from the Darwinian necessity of living life in a big city born and sustained through the parentage of capitalism. Saudis seem to eschew any sort of purpose-driven movement, opting instead for a leisurely meandering style, as if doing anything else would amount to a vulgar display of intention and would be considered poor taste. Friendly advice offered from a Saudi to any visiting Westerner often consists of this: If you want to blend in, friend, you must appear as if you have nowhere to go.

R&G's assessment of these two guys is confirmed when, as their paths are about to meet, part of their conversation is overheard: "Oh, yeah – no, dude, he'll walk. He's got himself a lawyer and everything, so…" And this snippet of conversation, along with the speakers' sketchy bearing, are enough to set the imaginations of both Gallagher and Rogarth alight, as neither of them have been, especially in their pre-AA lives, strangers to the United States legal system, especially as defendants for various drug-related offenses to society. The legal infraction that landed Rogarth inside the Cri-Life front doors four months ago grew from an extended visit to his parents' home in a privileged, albeit somewhat dusty and mountainous area about 100 miles north of Los Angeles, in a part of the state well outside the progressive sphere of influence of the great megalopolis, and therefore not open to the idea of providing needle exchanges for its dope-injecting-and-therefore-prone-to-catching-blood-borne-bugs-kind of citizen, which Rogarth doesn't really give two shits about, mainly because he's been aware of his HIV status for years already. The needle exchanges in LA were simply a means to obtain brand new (read sharp and unclogged) rigs that, given the amount of product Rogarth and his friends injected into their veins, preserved their epidermises with as little damage as possible. Before new needles were readily available to the impaired masses, their arms resembled pepperoni sausages.

Which begs the question: Why did Rogarth want to visit his parents in the first place?

A: Good intentions.

Like most folks on earth, dope fiends (even meth freaks) are prone, now and again, to fits of guilt, shame and regret, three states of mind that will, more often than not, evaporate well before the transformation from thought to deed. Once that threshold is crossed, however, the act gathers strength and momentum until, when perceived in the mind of the dope fiend, it turns into a full-blown act of what might be mistaken for caring and selflessness – or, objectively speaking, a truly domesticated understanding of the concept of "love," or more plainly, the currency on which about 1000 percent of Disney cartoons are built: I know he's monstrous…but I *love* him for what's inside his soul. Or in Rogarthian terms: I know I've been a horrible son. I've stolen your money and possessions, I've taken advantage of your feelings for me and I've ruined the reputation of our family. But I love you more than you can know, and I'm here to make amends.

Further objectivity, however, will reveal that before this deed has a chance to mature or even see puberty, the reality sets in that Rogarth or James or Sally or whoever, once they realize they've left the safety of their natural habitats that includes quick access to their drugs, will begin to have second thoughts. Just prior to being tested by the stress created by the tortured trial-and-error baby steps of wide-eyed pedestrians – much less the rolling big rigs necessary to deliver the building blocks of renewal onto the loading dock of one's character – the road to hell falls into disrepair.

Only two days into Rogarth's arrival to his parents' Ojai home – and given Ventura County's lack of largesse, at least as it might relate to clean needles – Rogarth, who set out on this trip dopeless and rigless, found himself, mid-jones, loitering through the halls of the local hospital, surreptitiously opening various drawers looking for syringes, a strategy which illustrates the cunning of the addicted mind, given the fact that, in his formative years, he'd had numerous dope connections, including his supervisor at one of the rare jobs he'd been able to secure in his lifetime. Valery, the head waitress of the Ojai Valley Inn, an overly popular patrician getaway, had spilled the beans to him one night after the dinner shift by uttering the word Desoxyn into the phone loudly enough to be overheard by Rogarth, who, emboldened by his knowledge that Desoxyn, better known as pharmaceutical methamphetamine (the kind, it was rumored, used by Adolph Hitler himself and was still prescribed now and then to regular non-fascist folks in order to ward off the effects of narcolepsy and sometimes epilepsy) was a rare term used only by certain physicians, pharmacists and, of course, dope fiends, who coveted this particular form of meth because its preparation for injection didn't involve any flames or spoons, and is so pure that it can be skin-popped, which is great if your arms have undergone the inevitable vein drain that most dope fiends experience after decades of stabbing their epidermises where they've predicted a vein lays because prediction, since plain old eyesight, due to misshapen eyeballs and lenses that are the result of too many awesome rushes, is all you have left in your quest for viable conduits. Rogarth had asked Valery about it, to which she at first blanched, then grinned, telling him that she wanted them to get high together, at which time Valery would slip on a pair of steel high heels, squeeze into a leather bustier, and then beat the shit out him. So Rogarth, after opting *not* to give Miss Valery a call, immediately pocketed a couple of hospital syringes large enough to be labeled harpoons, as well as an unopened vial of epinephrine, something he'd never tried and never even considered, but what the hell, was being handcuffed by one of the local sheriff's deputies for multiple legal transgressions. How such a seemingly minor offense, especially in California, warranted, in terms of seriousness, any more than a ceremonial appearance inside a courtroom resulting in a sentence greater than a bit of community service, was simply because this was a road not unknown to Rogarth, who'd nearly burned through the maximum number of minor offenses for which anything but state prison was appropriate punishment in the minds of defense attorneys and prosecutors alike.

During a quick and illuminating (at least for Rogarth) conversation with his assigned public defender, Judi Goldberg, Esq., a thirty-something barrister with the physical attributes of an overstuffed Barcalounger Pegasus II with a short, stylish haircut, Rogarth, wanting to show off both his legal acumen and his will to fight the system, raised his palm facing Mme. Goldberg's cherubic face and interjected his desire for her to "cut to the chase" and run a 1538.5 motion at his preliminary hearing, a strategy that, if successful, would have forced We The People's representative on earth to discard the evidence they'd garnered in order to secure a conviction. Better known as a motion to suppress, a 1538.5 motion is like a throw-away camera: it's something that can be used only once during the entire life of a legal case and, because of details like the burden of proof (a hot potato that imbues the prosecution with complete tactical advantage), has about as much chance of succeeding as the proverbial snowball in hell. Ms. Goldberg, having seen maybe not "all of it before," but a lot of it, responded with a musical quality to her voice that was as close to singing as speaking could be: "That…would open up a whole *can* of worm," a style of speech she picked up from one Bernie Fierro, her flaming yet distinguished legal mentor whose conversational dissents regarding outmoded and thus feeble arguments often included the phrase, "_That_, my dear, is positively antediluvian," where the "u" would elongate, soar and linger in the air as if part of a Puccini aria, along with her seemingly intentional use of the singular "worm," not only struck Rogarth silent mid-thought, but opened wide what was left of the corroded floodgates of his meth-addled brain. With mercurial speed, his imagination conjured a tiny movie trailer that featured his lawyer, dressed in a plush yet matted terrycloth robe, at home with several feline companions at her feet, opening a can labeled "Pâté of Worm," scooping out several spoonfuls and frying them in Canola oil, and then, selfishly avoiding the cats completely, depositing them carefully onto a burgundy-colored Melmac plate, then sitting at her kitchen table, sprinkling them with salt and pepper and chowing down, a meal that amounted to, unlike Pope Leo X's 1520 denunciation of Martin Luther's radical anti-Catholic principles, literally a diet of worms. That, along with the fact that it was apparent to Rogarth that her analogy was faulty; that rather than opening up a whole can of "worm" or "worms" (or taking the first misguided step down the slippery slope of ruin), Ms. Goldberg should have equated the running of a 1538.5 motion with the choice of whether to open up one's Christmas presents on Christmas Eve or Christmas morning, the former having the ability to spoil the surprise, the net effect of which was what Christmas presents were all about anyway; that what she really should be emphasizing to Rogarth was the virtues of patience rather than the shock and awe of spilling her strategic beans prematurely. After his thought ended with the quick assessment of Ms. Goldberg's girth, Rogarth found himself mildly surprised and amused by the fact that worms, apparently, were as fattening as cupcakes. So, finding himself confused and distressed by both his lawyer's seeming inability to grasp the distinction between things plural and a processed collective whole, along with her perceived penchant for eating insects, something that he, almost as a side thought, correlated with the fact that she had a Jewish last name: I knew it, they eat worms! – a suspicion that bolstered, one more time, the walls separating Gentiles and Jews, Rogarth, right there on the spot, surrendered and said he wanted to plead guilty and request a program.

In what can best be described as a pro forma process, Rogarth, after affixing his signature to the essential documents that sealed his fate and served as the roughage that propelled his journey through the bowels of the legal system with unobstructed speed, was surrendered to a representative of the previously mentioned Cri-Life Recovery House, the price for which was paid with a minimum of time spent incarcerated behind bars. It was, according to just about everybody in the State, one more time, a win-win proposition.

CHAPTER THREE

To say that Bert should have known that choosing to sell meth was probably not the soundest strategy to traverse middle age is easy to say when you're separated by a certain distance from deed or consequence: He should have known better. Or saying that Korn should have known that buying and moving into a house in this almost exclusively Jewish neighborhood twenty-two months ago would have upset a certain balance – actually stirred up ancient fears and all manner of potent forces. How could he have known that just showing up here would have amounted to a mindless clipping of the DNA strands that caused his new neighbors to, however unconsciously – as if any Jew could forget, if even for a moment, the hatred, or the fear, or the hatred, whichever shore you're planting your flag on – to overlook the basis of Jewish identity as made manifest by either Golgotha or the Shoah, when a non-Jew appears, closes escrow and moves in across the street from the Cohens and the Glicks, between the Silversteins and the Coopers. How could he have known that the dogwood tree adorning the front yard of Rabbi Perlmutter, who lives just next door to Chayim Silverstein, was a rabid expression of revenge: *You thought it hurt the first time? Just wait!* It's unrealistic. So even if many of the longtime residents on Kenmore Avenue had been able to rely on civility and manners instead of allowing a certain view of history – one more time – to shape their reaction to the introduction of a Gentile into their mostly well-tended, upper class neighborhood of single-family dwellings with front yards and clean unobstructed sidewalks, the fact that Korn and almost all his friends were gay, were infected with HIV/AIDS, and rarely slept because their appetites for methamphetamine – both using and selling – found them tending gardens, washing cars, and converting the gray, monolithic slab of concrete driveway into a melismatic mosaic of broken glass and gum drops that was brilliant in both its fractal detail and lack of planning, at three in the morning, sealed their fate.

On the other hand, maybe the Jewish residents *should have known* that Korn and friends posed no threat to them at all. But how could they have known? How could they have known that gay meth freaks don't consider much of anything except the following:

1. This would be pretty here.
2. Why isn't my dick hard?
3. That guy's hot.
4. When does Home Depot close?
5. Who're they and why are they watching me?
6. Why isn't my dick hard?

So it's little wonder that Korn, caught up in his preoccupation with what rests between his legs along with the ephemera literally centimeters before him, came to a convenient understanding that his neighbors' seeming lack of curiosity about him and his household was proof that he was invisible and not capable of eliciting a neighborly "hello" now and then from the Silversteins or the Glicks, was as short-sighted and incorrect as the decision to include a well-intentioned but impossibly vague guarantee of the pursuit of happiness in this country's founding documents. It's only with the gift of hindsight that it becomes apparent that one would endow victimhood with the status of legitimate political class, and the other would lend tacit approval to a household of felons. This pantomime of indifference was, in reality, the only mechanism, short of murder, available for the good people of South Kenmore Avenue to symbolically band together, along with every conceivable municipal entity willing to listen, and prepare to perform the surgery necessary to rid this neighborhood of its newest arrivals, even though, given the attitudes toward gay people in the best of circumstances, murder was probably the favored solution, especially since the traditions shaping the beliefs of the Kenmore Avenue Jews grew from that wellspring of progressive ideals known as The Bronze Age. As recently as 1976, it was illegal in The Golden State to butt fuck somebody – but in California's defense, the anti-sodomy laws here never singled out homosexuals, but instead enjoined all its residents from cavorting down any anal canal at all. But gay dope dealers was another story.

Mere weeks after Korn moved in, his neighbors were communicating with narcotics officers of the LAPD about the unsavory people and illegal activities taking place near their precious children.

And it's not like Korn, or any of the half dozen or so permanent residents or myriad visitors here would have offered much resistance to even a stern lecture delivered by the Pharisees of Kenmore Avenue either, and much less to a straight-up shakedown by the uniformed black-and-whites of some Narcotics Division. They're as substantial as a bouquet of crystalline dandelions with virtual hardons – "virtual" because one thing about meth freaks: they might be wasting away from a diet of AIDS medications and Gatorade, but they're horny as fuck and engorged with unflagging enthusiasm, which is a pretty poor substitute for the malingering blood cells who're finding it a bit of a challenge to congregate inside a penis – to finally clasp hands and perform a river dance, for which the most accurate adjective to describe the product of their work might be "malleable." It's called meth-dick, a workaday frustration that we've all learned to live with. Actually, there seems to be another opinion about this condition, whether it might be more accurate to name it "psychology dick" rather than meth dick. The correlation between meth use and soft penises, some might say, doesn't amount to a straight-up cause-and-effect, but rather is the product of endless complication, mentally speaking, which is itself a product of meth use and the failure or inability to compartmentalize: This isn't a sex club, it's merely a trip to Safeway to buy kibble for Fluffy; this isn't a meticulously planned fifth column street force preparing to attack your front door, it's merely the neighbors arriving home from Ralphs; that guy isn't a horny straggler from that uniform/leather bar down on Hyperion, he's just the mailman – and about one thousand other similar examples of misplaced horniness or paranoia, one of the minor effects of which results in the constricted capillaries that will wilt even the highest octane hardons. Meth use, as opposed to say the exponentially more essential and delimiting qualities of heroin, which, when all is said and done, weaves its crucial fictions around the simple binaries of life/death, awake/asleep, ecstasy/pain, and locates sexual activity on the same stratum as tying one's shoes, seems to lie in a much more easily acceptable form that rests on the bedrock of capability: even though you've done nothing but masturbate in front of the TV for the past three days, usually settling out of laziness on the Discovery Channel, the meth high transforms the perception of the greasy mundane into the much more lofty heights of accomplishment. Just as nearly 100 percent of spiders (and probably tons of various birds as well), which are constantly in the process of either spinning their webs or building their nests, meth heads are likewise constructing their own constantly changing contexts into which to fit new and different versions of themselves. It's a trick – an ingenious trick born of biology, pharmacology and more than a few survival tricks spanning millennia – that affords the meth user the ability to construct for himself a new and plausible life story at exactly the same time that he's escaping from a previous one – and can, and often does, occur multiple times within a twenty-four-hour period, which is a condition that makes you wonder why meth use isn't immediately excised from various Penal Codes around the country and having it placed into the pantheon of behaviors that have earned a perch into the rarified category of civic virtue, because it's pretty obvious that meth users create perfect consumers: profligate spenders who are known to dump mountains of cash – whether it's earned through legitimate methods or, what's more than likely the case, theft of property or selling dope – on stuff they don't even need – because shopping, after all is said and done, is definitely an activity – and, objectively speaking, is more closely related to masturbation than say carburetor repair, which isn't exactly brain surgery, but is still far outside most dope fiends' wheelhouse of expertise. Meth use is popular in the United States of America precisely because of the Puritan work ethic upon which the union was formed. It offers the illusion of getting things done. It's impossible to imagine a scenario where meth use would ever gain a foothold in Greece or Spain or France, where enjoyment of the midday nap and the appreciation of a sweet afternoon breeze are paramount.

The diabolical (and wonderful) qualities of drug use, though, (both opiates and amphetamines) are that it begins with the unassailable truth that obstacles of both the imagination and the spirit are rendered mere details easily vanquished by the drug. The housewife can do more with less; the artist can see further; the impoverished can easily accept that nirvana is just around the corner. Even though he probably never used meth, Plato understood the paradox of addiction: meth is the medicine that makes life bearable, and is, at the same time, the poison that destroys it.

The reality is that no one has partied here for about a year. The magic furnished so generously at the beginning of drug use had long since turned the corner toward the drudgery of routine. Korn's place has eroded into a household of errand-runners, scoring meth, doing chores and beginning projects. Lots to do! Gotta run! The washing machine and drier are constantly churning out towels and more towels, more like a hospital than a home. It's as if the trousseaux accompanying the five or so permanent residents here at Korn's house consist not of jeweled tiaras or oversized broaches from this or that grandmother (who had a hunch that little Andy either takes it up the butt now or presently will be), but stack upon stack of terrycloth towels dragged from one temporary *domicile fixe* to another – stuffed into trash bags, the *de rigueur* default luggage of convenience for an entire social class consisting of those (mostly) gay men who contracted HIV/AIDS at a time when it was a death sentence, and a social class that both fueled and benefited from the metastatic growth, both medically and politically, of the epidemic. Even if Korn and company had wanted to jump off the AIDS bandwagon, they were stuck – along for the twenty-five-year HIV hayride that at first defined them as pathetic victims with weeks of breath left inside their lungs, then brave survivors, and finally what the fuck ever, you're probably gonna live to be a hundred if you eat right, take your meds, exercise, vote and perform most of the mountain of activities used to define a virtuous citizenry. So welcome to life, motherfucker! Either get with the program, get to work, and live loud; or wither and die. It's no wonder that Korn and his buddies chose something else.

CHAPTER FOUR

I really like hearing these three words: Be safe, Bert. I mean, really. Be safe. It's us against them. At three in the afternoon or three in the morning, standing in the doorway, getting ready to leave with a lengthy jail sentence locked tight in a leather case or tucked casually in a front pocket or camouflaged like a half-eaten hamburger inside a grease-stained paper sack, I always wait to hear those reassuring words: Travel safe; be safe. Resist the urge to stay here. It's not safe. This house has been glowing, undulating with its fecund taunt for months now: We're here and we're ready to be shaken down and harvested like so much illegal fruit. The delay can make you crazy. What are the police waiting for? It'll be dark soon. Be safe out there. And I realize that whoever tells me this might actually believe that I have the wherewithal to stay ahead of the law – to be safe. The words make me feel good – well, better anyway, as I subscribe to the fiction that I've fooled somebody into believing that making it home uncaught has anything to do with circumstances beyond pure chance, as I gauzily view myself as formidable – as a guy with a plan who can actually drive the fourteen miles home holding a half-ounce of crystal meth somewhere on my person without a hitch. So I wait for Korn to say the words, but instead this is what I hear: "Hang out for a minute." The invitation is impossible to turn down, and I know isn't made lightly. It almost always means that the stores of meth are dry for the moment, and that the "minute" referred to could mean an hour or a week.

CHAPTER FIVE

Inertia: a property of matter by which it continues in its existing state of rest or uniform motion in a straight line, unless that state is changed by an external force.

The part of this definition that describes the dope fiend – gay or straight – better than the approximately hundred trillion pages of well-intended method by which addicts or alcoholics can veer away from their destinations of doom are the words *straight line. Just turn a little bit. Take a day off…five minutes, for Christ's sake.*

Bending the straight line requires either novelty and imagination, or the brute force that's embodied by a set of handcuffs and a night stick. Shame, to the uninitiated, might seem like just the ticket to cause a dope fiend to change course. But that's a load of shit. Just ask Janice, whose kids, for years were served breakfast bowls of corn flakes swimming in tap water instead of milk because money reserved for milk was diverted to the dope fund – and kids being their own adorable, needy selves, what are they going to do about it anyway, besides cry? Or Richard, who would have lost his arm abscessed from shooting impure dope into muscle instead of a vein, to gangrene had it not been for the colony of ants who, sensing a generous store of nourishment festering nearby, marched in columns up his arm and down again as he lightly snored for several blissful hours under a nod of smack, and outside to feed their winter colony disgusting albeit delicious meals of pus.

An argument could be made that dope fiends are ultimately motivated by a need for chaos. That sounds pretty good, and seems like it would have quite a lot of support. But it's not chaotic. Chaos is just the first step in a process that quite quickly erodes into the tiniest, narrowest crevice where every exit is blocked by craving and fear of being outdoors, just you and your habit. There's an exquisite vulnerability to this state of being. Burroughs described it really well. But it's not chaotic and it's not noble. It's just selfish. And not the kind of selfish where kids are stingy about sharing their popsicles or their toys or their affection. It's selfish with capital hyphenated letters – the kind of selfish that flies into the sun because you don't have the wherewithal to see that any current circumstances will even slightly satisfy your tremendous appetites, so you just keep going, doing the same thing over and over again. Given enough time around dope fiends, though, people begin to see patterns emerging: The chaos of unrestrained appetite evolves (dissolves) into order, but it's usually an imposed order courtesy of the State. And over time this pattern repeats, and repeats again until enough time passes that the state loses interest because the dope fiend, just like everybody else on earth, is dead.

What motivates dope fiends is fear…or something.

CHAPTER SIX

Day 1: Cri-Life Recovery House, Victory Boulevard, North Hollywood, California.

Cri-Life, being one of the only facilities in the universe that prides itself on being what's characterized in its self-promoting marketing pamphlets as "not just gay friendly, but gay *sensitive*," caters to an inordinately high number of gay men and women, a condition that, when viewed through squinty eyes, an-only-slightly-less-intentioned-than-effortless effort that helps to obscure the difference in appearance between convict and cop; butcher and baker; dancer and singer; male and female; homo and hetero; obese and emaciated, makes Cri-Life, Inc. one hell of a diverse place.

The House staff, in an attempt to be fair, size up each new resident with the same process: the arrival room where newcomers are strip searched for contraband contains both a single carafe Mr. Coffee machine as well as a seventy-five-gallon (approximately) metal brewing vat that warms the same batch of coffee in twenty-four-hour increments. Even though most new arrivals need a cup of coffee about as much as Mother Teresa needed IUDs, they almost always make a beeline for the stack of Styrofoam cups sitting between the two machines, and not being complete morons (usually), they will opt for the Mr. Coffee instead of the institutional vat of warm bile, and pour themselves a portion of freshish coffee which immediately confiscated by employees of the facility known as *technicians* or *techs* for short, an act that's accompanied with the pronouncement: Everything You Know Is Wrong, along with the explanation that the Mr. Coffee coffee is for staff while residents must drink what's in the vat. The next few seconds are crucial, and serve as a pretty good gauge that predicts how well or how unwell each new resident will fare during his/her stay at the House of Cri: He will hopefully, docilely, or with a minimum of protest, surrender the fresher coffee and drink the bile.

But Rogarth said the forbidden word: *"But…"*

And it really doesn't matter what follows the italicized conjunction. Considerations social, medical, spiritual, emotional, physical are all lumped into the same trash heap of thought that must be banished from the mind *tout de suite*. This, as they say, is just the nipple of the teat of wisdom that governs almost 100 percent of recovery houses extant in the USA: This is not a democracy. We don't care about your opinions because your opinions are – how to put this lovingly – shit. And we know they're shit because – well, just look where you are. Even though the circular nature of this logic is discerned by some new arrivals, many of them happily relinquish their critical thinking skills along with their deluxe coffee and deport most of their opinions to some kind of weird purgatory in the backs of their heads, an unsurprising process because it quickly becomes apparent, even to the blind person, that living in this recovery house is about one trillion times better than rotting inside a jail cell. And to those experienced at being inmates, the concept of time behind bars is ever present in the decision-making part of the brain: this is a six-month program, tops – and I can probably spend seven months doing pirouettes and *pliés* while balancing on the head of a glowing hot straight pin, so fuck it.

"…*But…* I want *that* coffee."

"Is that *all* you want?"

"Huh? No – I" –

"Everything You Know Is Wrong."

"It's just coffee."

"The alternative is death or jail."

"For the coffee?"

"Maybe you'd like to wait here while I call your probation officer."

"Never mind."

###

BE SAFE

Rogarth was escorted upstairs with his scant luggage and sack of toiletries and into his third story dorm room by Michael (Mike) Gallagher, who, by virtue of his arrival to Cri-Life twelve weeks earlier, had been assigned the task of showing Rogarth around. The room, a misshapen gray parallelogram with offset door at the front and a weird concession to a bay window at the opposite end complete with a trapezoidal bench *sans* cushion and hinge because that would create hiding places for contraband, which includes everything from the felonious drug and/or cell phone, to the less serious transgressions of pizza slice and/or soda cracker or green apple – all the way to misdemeanor possession of non-Cri-Life-approved literature, which is any writing not Recovery-oriented and/or Jesus-slanting – basically any reading material not of the type that might be furnished by Jehova's Witnesses. The view out the bay window is just the over-worked AC units mounted on the roof of an adjacent building, which keep the temperature in Rogarth's room at the meat-hanging degree. The entire floor – all residential floors – are, for the moment, deserted and enjoying a rare state of calm. It's a serious infraction to exist on any residential floors during the day except for anomalous occurrences, like recuperating from a minor illness – "minor" being the operative word because there exists in most recovery facilities an overt readiness to refuse service to anyone seriously handicapped: *We just aren't equipped to deal effectively with his/her condition* – or showing new people the ropes.

As the mentor in the room, Gallagher valiantly tries to come off all enthusiastic about the prospect of sobriety and second chances, and Rogarth, the newcomer, valiantly tries to come off like the interested pupil, even though what's gnawing at the tail end of both their thoughts at the moment is that they've found themselves – one more time – confronting the implicit expectations that institutions like Cri-Life have about their residents: becoming comfortable with the notion of living long and meaningful lives, drug and crime free, especially since AIDS has conditioned both of these guys to living on the installment plan from one blood test to the next. And whether they know it or not, drug use has helped to obscure this reality. Gallagher points to his bed, which is the closest to the bay window.

"You can have any bed except that one. That's where I sleep."

"Cool, thanks."

"Because you're new, you can take a nap before dinner."

"When's that?"

"In about forty-five minutes. That's 4:30...every day except Sunday and Saturday."

"What time then?"

"About when you get hungry – it's pretty casual on weekends, 'casual' being relative term. What kind of a name is Rogarth?"

"I don't know. My teachers always said it was a name of significant potential. I'm not so sure though."

"You wanna stay clean?"

"Who knows."

"Rogarth, sweetie, you gotta make a decision. At least pretend for a while, or you're not gonna make it here."

"Yeah. I'm remembering now how to do it: Get grateful. *I'm grateful for the shoes on my feet, I'm grateful for my feet; I'm grateful for the cars on the streets, I'm grateful for streets.* Nice to meet you. I'm not really such an asshole most of the time."

"No problem. Welcome to Cri-Life. My first name's Mike – but I go by Gallagher."

"Hey, Gallagher, thanks."

"Where you from?"

"Hollywood. Where else."

"Right? Smoking's on the patio. They catch you smoking up here, we're all fucked."

"My lawyer said this place is totally cool with gay guys."

"That part is true. There's a ton of us with AIDS – oh, sorry. I guess I assumed that since they chose me to show you around that there must be a common denominator."

"Yeah, I got it too."

"What drug they have you on?"

"Some cocktail. Rayataz or some shit and a couple more."

"Let me give you some good advice.

"'Good' advice?"

"Yeah, about being here and having AIDS."

"Sure."

"We're not special. Really. I can tell you that every person here that I know of who's got AIDS has pretty much the same story when it comes to a shitty plateau of behavior. All of us have used it – when I say 'it' I mean every little bit of shit you can squeeze out of the virus in order to get some leverage with your family and friends and shit. Ring a bell? *Oh, I'm really sorry I robbed that liquor store – I was just so distraught because I probably only have three weeks left before – you know. Or please mom and dad, all I need is $6,000 for an experimental protocol in Switzerland – it covers airfare and everything – that's only available to three more people – or I might die really soon.* We've *all* done it, so I'm just telling you this so that if you might be afraid you'll be judged if you share that kind of shitty behavior in group, just know it's something we've all done. You believe in god?"

"Oh, the god thing."

"Yeah. You kinda have to believe in god here. It's in a few of the Steps; *Made a decision to turn our will and our lives over to the care of God as we understood* him, which is the biggie, but it's also in the previous step too, but in that one, god comes at you a little sideways – it's one of the sneakier steps because it assumes you're already relying on god, where in the next step the whole question of belief is tackled. And even though the folks here stress that it's a god of your understanding who you need to get right with, they always, like it's some automatic huge rubber band, snap you right back to the Christian god with the Ten Commandments and the prostrating yourself before the blinding glorious light of redemption. They can't help it. And you can't really blame 'em because look around. This place is like the opposite of a college campus where complicating the fuck out of everything is what you do. This is Cri-Fucking-Life, so only slightly more complicated than county jail. You can't blame anybody for trying to force you to believe in something – it's just kind of the expedient. They've only got six or seven months to turn your head around, and relying on some kind of god to get you through the day is better than relying on the LAPD. They're okay with it if you decide that your god is maybe the door knob in your room or something – that kind of stuff is great for the first month or so, but sooner or later they expect you to come around to Christianity with Jesus and salvation. And if you say you're an atheist, forget about it. That shit totally makes their heads explode – like to them it opens a door that lets them show you how deep they can think: *So, you think you're the most powerful force in the universe,* they'll say, and by example, they'll pull out their logic guns and aim them right at your temple: *So, Mr. All Powerful, why don't you just head down to the beach and order the waves to stop rolling in. How powerful do you think you are now?* Or a favorite line of attack goes something like this: The CDW asking the questions will hold up two fingers or point to two cigarette butts or something, and ask, *Rogarth, if you add two fingers to two more fingers, how many fingers would you then have?* Give him the answer, but delay it a little bit, like to show that you're trying to figure out his strategy. Say, *Four fingers,* but retain a befuddled look on your face and let him continue. The next question will go something like this: *Rogarth, do unicorns exist?* And your answer will be something like, *Of course unicorns don't exist!* He's on a roll now. Let him go for it. He'll say: *Ok, cool. We can agree that unicorns don't exist. Rogarth, if you add two unicorns to two more unicorns – knowing that they actually don't exist – how many unicorns would you then have?* He's not really waiting for you to add two and two together again – he's waiting for you to experience a life-changing revelation about the nature of faith – as if adding unicorns or werewolves or vampires rather than fingers or cigarette butts requires a profound willingness to believe in the unseen – actually the unseeable – rather than the grease spot of rigor required to simply perform a basic mathematical abstraction. Just let your mouth fall open – get all sappy and agape and grateful looking, like you've been struck by lightning from heaven, and say something like *Golly! I never thought of it that way. Thank you!* – just go along for the Bible ride while you're here, Rogarth. Rick's your CDW?"

"Yeah…"

"Mine too. He used to be the go-to guy for AIDS residents, but there's so many of us now, we get spread between Rick and Diane T., who's pretty cool even though she's AIDS-free. Her AIDS cherry popped when she started dating some guy named Leonard T., who they say passed on about ten years ago from AIDS-related stuff. But Rick's got most of us. He's an asshole…he runs the HIV support group on Saturday. The gang-bangers hate it that we get out of double-scrub to talk about the butt flu."

"His teeth are" –

"Yeah, I know. Intense. I'll take you down to the dining room later. You should knock out for a while if you want."

"Yeah, thanks. I'm fucking beat. Hey…can I ask you something?"

"Depends."

– Gallagher lies on his bed. –

"Do *you* believe in god, Gallagher?"

"Don't know. My turn. You really wanna be sober?"

"You mean outside of here? Because it's kind of obvious that, *in here*, you kind of need to at least pretend you want to be sober. I mean, that's what's going on here, right? Everybody is pretending they want to be sober? And even the people who run this place – like Rick – they're probably aware that most people are just pretending – like some elaborate theater production, but a few of 'em will probably still be pretending even years from now. So I'm good with saying that I'm good with pretending to want to be sober, and to want to believe in god."

"It doesn't matter right at the moment I don't think. There's some good people here though."

"That's cool."

"There's a shit-load of assholes too."

"Like Rick."

"Yeah…there's a way to get him to spin like a motherfucker."

"Tell me."

"He's gotta be really insecure. Just mention something you did once that's like pretty cool…like even if it's not true, say you met Igor Stravinsky or Stephen Hawking or something one time, like he was maybe friends with your grandmother or whatever. And Rick can't stand it. He's gotta one-up you, like it turns into a bona fide arms race, but instead of missiles and tanks, it's always how high class he is compared to everybody else in the USA. He'll say that the exiled Queen Jadwiga of the Polish royal family is friends with his parents and actually ate dinner at their house one time up in Sand Canyon or some shit, like ten years ago he actually had a conversation with a real legitimate queen, which, in his mind, is better than eating dinner with just about anybody including the president or maybe Aaron Copeland or somebody like that, like there's absolutely no room for dissent. And the interesting thing is how sly he thinks he's being when he tells you this stuff, like he'll maybe compliment your shirt or something, and then, like it makes total sense after you say 'thank you,' he'll say that this Polish queen 'gifted' him a shirt that was similar to your shirt – and he really will say 'gifted' instead of 'gave' – almost like a smart-alecky fifth grader who's showing off in class. And if you ask what it is his father does for a living that warrants a visit from Queen Jadwiga in the first place, he'll look right at you and he'll smile with those teeth and that tan – and he'll just say his dad's a lawyer, but in a way designed to make you believe that you might as well banish any thoughts about public defenders or assistant DAs or any kind of local politics from your mind right away, because this kind of lawyer is pretty rarified. And you can see that he's studying you to see if the wheels in your brain are conjuring the correct tableaux that show maybe palaces in Poland, or cloisonné aviaries inside some Middle East floating city with magical mechanical birds that actually fly even though it was built in the Middle Ages, or maybe the White House with butlers and heads of state and his dad and mom all dressed in tuxedos and gowns, bowing and kissing people on their cheeks, like it's just so goddamned high class and *waaay* beyond your comprehension. And he must practice this shit a lot, because when he ran this line of crap on me, he like steered my thoughts – or at least fed me enough information and the right kind of information that I never even, for a second, considered that any of his family were Republicans or people that you usually equate with wealth, but are instead rich Democrats, which, you gotta admit, is a ton cooler than just being rich conservative assholes who're all pale and doughy and who never see any sunlight, like all they do is pull wings off of insects or something in a darkened inner sanctum somewhere – which plays right into Rick's whole *I'm-the-coolest-motherfucker-here* line of crap. And it starts to make sense, his teeth and everything and his muscles and his tan, all that *'just so'* bullshit. But he keeps his cool, you know, even though he just can't fucking wait for you to ask him a question about his past, like 'wow, what did you study in school,' or something like that, because I asked him that and he, just like it was nothing at all, said, 'I'm a lawyer – I have a degree in law, actually, but I've never actually *practiced* law.' I guess this is designed to get you to think that practicing law or anything else is beneath him; like he's here at Cri-

Life due to his following some altruistic code or something – which is weird when you think about it because he's always quoting Ayn Rand to people on his caseload who've shirked their responsibilities – like there was a secret beacon like the one Batman sees in the night sky that summoned him to come to North Hollywood and save everybody."

"Wow – a fag with AIDS who quotes Ayn Rand."

"Like he can't see that you're aware that this is so much bullshit, like you've never heard the term cognitive dissonance before, much less the fact that anybody who *really digs* Ayn Rand would never be caught dead working in a place like this, like if it was Ayn Rand World here, dope fiends – especially dope fiends with AIDS – would be either locked up or shot or just left to die on the side of the road or something. Like you want to just ask him if he ever used dope at all, or if he's just here doing some kind of dissertation or something. Maybe that's it. Maybe he never really enjoyed being high – I mean not like *I* did – or probably you did, or most of the people here did. I mean I fucking *love* dope. I love it as much as religious guys say they love Jesus. Shooting meth was my religion. I love everything about it: the way it looks, how it's packaged, how *illegal* it is, the penalties you have to pay for using it, how you can martyr yourself to the cause. Maybe Rick enjoyed it for like maybe just a few days – or even a few hours – and he felt threatened by it, like he just couldn't let himself enjoy the high, like some guys think it's all about the sex, that they only use when they're getting laid, like they're actually, deep down, ashamed that they use drugs, and they put everything off on the sex, like that's the reason they're getting high in the first place."

"Sex is great."

"Sex is a place holder – something you do in between doses. I mean, when all is said and done, it's the drugs that I like – the ritual of everything – and the high, of course. Especially when I first started slamming the shit into my veins when I had decent veins, damn! How much fun was that! I used to love to jack off with the register, just to show off, you know, when you draw up some blood and it's really easy because your veins are pretty much pristine, and you push the blood back in and draw it up again and again – just like jacking off. And if you're really good, you can push a little bit more of the drug in each time you push it down. I love that shit. I bet that would have freaked the hell out of Rick."

"Could be."

"When they told him that AIDS probably wasn't going to kill him, he was probably all relieved and shit and probably said 'Thank god,' and drove to the nearest AA meeting. You can't point out to him that he's probably just a pussy who didn't really enjoy getting high."

"Because that would piss him off. You don't want to piss off the boss."

"You gotta stick to the Cri-Life recovery narrative. You gotta keep your CDW happy. You gotta keep 'em all happy."

"Okay."

"One more little bit of advice. You gotta work the Twelve Steps here – I've only been here for a little over two months, but here's the thing. When you get to Step Four, which is writing down all the shitty things you've ever done that you feel guilty about, when you read that list to your sponsor, you have to cry. If you don't cry, you'll have to stay on First Phase or Second Phase, which means you have to stay here on the premises all the time – no weekend passes or anything, which would really suck, so" –

"Remember to cry."

"Yeah. Because Rick will call your sponsor to find out if you cried or not."

"Gotcha."

"Because it's supposed to be cathartic, like confessing your sins to a priest."

"Or taking a shit."

"Exactly. There's a few guys you need to stay away from too. You'll see who they are. Really loud. Really amazingly annoying. There's a couple of guys who're here from some prison up north, they're like gargoyles. They hate gay guys, but they so don't want to get sent back up state for being anti-gay – there's this whole *You-need-to-respect-everybody-here-no-matter-who-they-are-or-what-they've-done-because-everybody-deserves-a-chance* doctrine that Rick and all the CDWs really take seriously here, so these two guys – Robert #1 and Robert #2 – they're both named Robert. Robert #1 is good-looking and kind of slender with a ton of tattoos – and he's got some brains. I

41

stay away from him because I get the sense that he'd just as soon stab you as say hello, and he's totally unpredictable. But Robert #2 is interesting. I hung out with him in the med line once – he takes meds for some condition, like me, and I guess maybe you too, but I don't think he's got AIDS, but probably some kind of behavioral-type of drugs because – well you'll see – there's not much inside his skin beyond an on/off switch. Anyway, I'm standing right next to him and he's watching me read one of those announcements they tape to the window that says who's gotta go where, like doctor visits and going to court and the various times and shit. And I'd never strike up a conversation with somebody like Robert #2 because he's got bad skin and he's really short and fat and looks kinda like Quasimodo – they're a real couple, Robert #1 and Robert #2. Inseparable. But Robert #2's watching me read this announcement really closely, and he, just like we were friends or whatever, he comes up to me and says he doesn't know how to read. And I just look at him – I mean it's kind of obvious I'm not going to try to teach the guy to read while we're waiting in the med line – but the interesting thing is that he's not like upset or anything about this – he was kind of laughing when he told me this. But I asked him – because I right away wondered how he got through school – even like elementary school, because I thought everybody has to know a little bit of how to read to make it to high school. But I said something that sounded really fucking lame, like *Oh, really?* which isn't a real question but whatever. But he comes up to me and he seems sincere, but still kind of amused, and he points to the words in the sentences and he kind of like confesses to me that he's always been good with the *concept* of reading and comprehending words, like he knows there need to be words that signify things like 'dog' and 'apple' and 'pussy,' but what's always freaked him out were the spaces between the words, like he was completely freaked out by the spaces because he didn't know what was happening with them, like the boundaries of each word were like little cliffs you could fall off of that emptied out into black holes or whole areas of uncharted space that exist around and in back of the words, where the spaces lead to – like there was a whole universe with its own rules going on behind the words and the sentences. But the wholesale unknown of what lay beyond each word wasn't really his issue. Robert #2, being a good dope fiend, was completely okay with accepting that overdoses might kill you. He was okay with that kind of unknown, the really big stuff, which, in most dope fiends' minds, makes them sort of Explorer Scouts or whatever or heroes who cheat death on a regular basis – that whole line of bullshit that we're all guilty of – I mean, I would totally rather die of an overdose than maybe one of those old fashioned diseases like Kaposi's Sarcoma or pneumocystis pneumonia or some shit. Robert #2 was afraid of a much smaller part of the unknown, basically of not knowing how to act in the spaces between and what was going on in back of the words, and he was afraid he'd be made fun of – like there were people and governments – at least some kind of rules back there that he thought he needed to know so he could blend in and hang out without having to study to learn the rules, which makes sense, because he was probably afraid that there was like some kind of Code with all the rules governing all this unknown space behind the words, which it's pretty obvious would just compound Robert #2's problem, because he'd have to know how to read in order to make sense of the Code, unless it was like part of some kind of oral tradition, which makes as much sense as there being a written down Code with all these rules, but Robert #2 wasn't thinking about oral traditions versus written. And I totally got it, because I mean, I've been in that same spot so many times before. I think a lot of us have. Like remember the first time you dropped acid and went to a gay bar – or even if you didn't take any acid – and you felt like everybody was watching you, which they probably were, but that kind of scrutiny usually ended with a huge payoff, like getting a huge cock up your ass at the end of the night or whatever, which, if you're blazing on acid, even if you weren't a hundred percent homosexual at the beginning of the night, that kind of experience would have made you a true believer by the next day. And this confession by Robert #2 – not about taking cocks – but the whole being freaked out by reading thing made me think that this guy, if he wasn't so goddamned ugly, would be cool to hang out with. That and his other half, Robert #1, who's really a pretty scary dude, and he totally influences Robert #2, like about a hundred percent."

"Wow."

"I know. What do you say to something like that? I thought it was really interesting though. Hey, there's another guy that smells bad – a black guy who always wears a long black leather coat kinda like Neo's coat, no matter if it's cold or hot, and they say he never bathes, but he's got money because he's always got tons of cigarettes. He's from New York – he was a reggae singer in New York, kind of famous I think. But he's got a thing for Catholic priests – and if you're out of cigarettes, all you gotta do is tell him you're a priest and he'll buy you a whole carton of whatever kind of cigarettes you want."

"Cool."

"It's almost 4:30. Let's go eat."

CHAPTER SEVEN

It never occurs to me that people might rely on God to help them seek my ruin. It's a weird thought: *Please God, help me to smite Bert.* I know I'm not perfect by any stretch – even when described in a less than charitable terms my life can easily appear as no more than an endless series of mistakes. But god? It would be thrilling if it weren't actually happening to everybody here in Korn's house, which is going to include me in about ten seconds.

I hold my breath and enter. Korn shuts the front door quick and tells me to head back to the rear of the house where everybody hangs out. Even as recently as a few months ago Korn used to glance quickly up and down the street to see if the Glicks or the Silversteins were watching when he answered the front door – but he knows better now. They're always watching, which makes any hopeful admonishment from Korn or anybody else here to *be safe* pretty much a moot point now.

It's quiet inside. No music; no TV – just the muted jargon of water sloshing in the washing machine – a syncopated distracted rhythm that's only slightly more energetic than tapping your foot to the beat of some dance song from the Bee Gees, which makes the sound easy to ignore; and of course there's the constant low even hum of the drier. The distant sound of a metal spoon or fork clanks into the kitchen sink. It doesn't hit any errant dishes, just the porcelain of the sink. The vague sound of a guy crying somewhere way in the back, the sound muffled by multiple walls and furniture and whatnot.

People talk at the rear of the house, but because of its rambling design it's impossible to make out much more than fragments of a few sharply angled vowels and some accented plosives and fricatives, but no actual words. It's a sprawling ranch-style affair with room after room laid out in a naively generous manner that speaks to its provenance: that time in Los Angeles when city planning relied on simply the property of addition to shape its neighborhoods and its dwellings. There's so much money and so much land all you have to do is add a room or a half-acre of land…whatever strikes your fancy.

I walk toward the back. Jimmy S. is lying on the floor in the hallway asleep. But he's deep in spaz sleep meaning he's pretty much a scientific anomaly. Meth leaks out of his pores, which smells weird, and he jumps around when he sleeps like he's the poster child for the dangers of meth use: Don't Let This Happen To You. And everybody kind of knows that he's not jumping around because he's dreaming intense shit – I mean even if he *is* dreaming, which is doubtful, it's probably dreams about boring stuff like eating breakfast or slicing up bits of okra for dinner – nothing fun anyway. I feel kind of sorry him for a minute because all that jumping around is caused by burned out neurons because he's awake more than anybody in the universe and his poor brain connections just want to take a little ten-minute break, just a little breather. But then it's kind of annoying too, like I wonder what'd happen if the place got raided and the cops see him flopping around like that in the hallway. I wonder if seeing him in the middle of this bouncing around would facilitate an arrest of everybody, and if so, if they'd arrest him or call for the paramedics to wheel him away on a gurney. Or would everybody inside the house be arrested *en masse,* where the whole process could be boiled down into a process that's like a simple equation where there would be no difference in weight or importance between buyers/users or visitors and residents, like everybody here at Korn's house would be assigned the same role of integer no matter what their standing here was; whether they lived here or not, regardless of the degree of criminality influencing them. And the mathematical process – the work that math does like addition or multiplication – all that would equal the act of making an arrest. And all law enforcement – all the cops – would adhere to the rules of the inverse property of multiplication where each of six cops equals $1/6^{th}$ of an arrest in total, and then, invoking the identity property of multiplication, this number of cops is multiplied by four meth freak visitors plus one meth freak owner plus two meth freak renters equals one arrest times seven meth freaks, or each arrest would equal $1/7^{th}$ of an entire bust, or if some people, by virtue of standing or taste, would create a new and ever more complicated algorithm that would result in what might amount to more or fewer arrests or just arrests that have different levels of seriousness.

I step over Jimmy. I don't want to wake him – he's easier to take when he's unconscious, because I kind of don't want to hear about how much money he made at the Spotlight, that hustler bar where most of Hollywood's dowager empresses hang out and are willing to spend their monthly stipends on bargain cocktails and overpriced cocks hanging between the legs of over-aged prostitutes who've been banished eastward past La Brea because all the millennial youth seem to land in West Hollywood – and who in his right mind would choose Grandpa Walton over some teenager? Jimmy S. is over fifty, so whatever. Here's just a sample of Jimmy's prose style, which he'd posted on a homo hook-up site in order to entice some eligible swinging dicked youngster into an extended period of nasty butt-fucking:

Hey – Lol wtf just saying P.arty N' P.lay lovrvthe fack that I can saythatvn love my life at the same time I say lol tex message ohhh wait callll lol anyways love clouds but get to th point horned out – porNo Gay straight dude fantasy love it my topfav am sure xxctra lol in more then one –well hey crazy bread crumbs as a favorite in highschool lol Colton live life to say dsmm werar I a momas boys oooo lol Monique love her n say day onevlol new years lol fuck u knocknout –pingrr lol nkuckel our life's u–say can't oooo nonloco jutvubresf love ubmessage mebyeah easier 02-0
Smoke Yes, Drugs Often.
8", Cut, HIV don't know. Prefer meeting at: Your Place.

Jimmy comes off as a guy who is completely devoid of guile – not that he's not bright or completely uneducated, but more like somebody who was pretty straight forward, even if he didn't want to be. But posting something like this is pretty damned clever. Who could resist that? And really, if you weigh what the alternative might consist of – a recitation of academic achievements and theoretical bullshit that would only attract someone with an equally rigid stick up his ass, this is a pretty sweet little composition that would serve as the honey to lure any number of skateboard riding youths and whatnot out onto the pavement and into his bed sheets. He must have been higher than fuck when he wrote it though, because he's not a complete moron when he's not completely twacked. Note the HIV disclosure at the end of this missive: "don't know," which in many minds absolves the posting party of the responsibility of intent.

Jimmy's still a pretty good looking guy though – square jaw, red hair done in a low-grade pompadour on good days. And his body's still intact, meaning if you see him from a distance he might be mistaken for somebody who's maybe fifteen or even twenty years younger than he is, but as he gets closer and closer, what strikes you is that gravity is in the middle of an all-out assault on the tensile strength of his skin until he gets right up next to you, and then he just looks like a piece of driftwood in shrink-wrapped flesh-colored bed sheets. The worst part of Jimmy S. though is talking to him. He's one of those poor guys who's been stuck on the same sex rush since the first time he got high – really high – like back in the 1990s or even the '80s, and he squanders his entire high following the dictates of an enfeebled imagination, which amounts to seeing a pickup truck parked outside a house or even an apartment building during daylight hours and deducing that it portends wild, drug-fueled homosexual activity going on behind the walls, the reasoning being something like this:

Truck = man; parked outside a dwelling during daylight hours = shirked responsibility of a job = obviously completely twacked like you = either in the middle or at the end of a previous night's group sex, which has ebbed for the moment, so they would be happy to see a new piece of meat (like your own damned self) introduced into their orgy, so find a way to get inside, but do it quickly because your high won't last all day.

No one wants to be subjected to yet another one of these descriptions of sexual searching – they've earned a place in kind of a micro mythos on Kenmore Avenue – and anyplace else where Jimmy hangs out. For some reason I stop myself from muttering the words *Poor Jimmy* – it's so easy to judge somebody else, especially for doing stuff that you yourself are guilty of – at least mostly anyway. A lot of the meth addicts I know – including yours truly – have been stuck in that same endless sexual loop, but I must say that mine was imbued with a certain ironic quality from the get go.

I was dating this cute young blond – a barback at one of LA's more twisted bars called Plug. I loved that place for any number of reasons, but mostly because if Plug had had a motto, it would have been: *If you can't do it at Plug, you can't do it anywhere.* Anyway, I started seeing Billy on pretty much a regular basis – and for somebody with a practically non-existent cock in terms of size he was absolutely great sex. Billy and I conspired together about sexual fantasies, conjuring far-fetched scenarios where we'd insinuate ourselves into the lives of various men around town whose personas were shaped by their professions: Airline pilots, cops, construction managers, Muslim clerics – you get the picture – and making ourselves so desirable that sex with these men would just seem like the natural progression of things; that wild butt-fucking that might remain out of the ordinary in general would become inevitable with us. Even though our plans never matured past the conspiratorial stage, I'm pretty sure that this time with Billy planted the seeds that led to me waking up one morning dressed in black leather motorcycle jacket, high-heeled shoes and come-fuck-me fishnet black nylons and a slutty red skirt inside a confessional at St. Vibianes Cathedral, which is in Downtown LA. My recollection is spotty but I remember that I'd slammed a ton of meth early in the evening and headed off on foot for the Alameda Corridor, that engine of economic vitality for pretty much all of the Southland, and which is known to be populated on a twenty-four-hour basis by swarthy Hispanic workers who unload the never-ending river of freight trains laden with everything from Froot Loops to Chevrolets and who I believed I could entice into taking advantage of me. But there I was at about eight in the morning sitting in this confessional – just waking up and sweating like a pig. I have little recollection of exactly how I got myself inside the church, but I'm pretty certain that at the time my little foray into Catholic land – since up until that time 99.9 percent of the thresholds I'd crossed in my life had little to do with salvation or resurrection – or even sin for that matter. Even though in college I spent an impaired night in

Russell's apartment discussing the word *threshold* itself with a number of folks who fancied themselves members of the thinky class when really we were just high as fuck, because the 'h' in "threshold" seems to be doing double duty, forming the final member of the *sh* sibilant sound while at the same time it's also reported for the substantial duty of being the initial letter of *hold*: *thresh*/hold, which is like pretty much the opposite of the '*l*'-*heavy* proper name *Llewellen,* where the repeated '*l*'s are pretty much just decoration.

I remember that just being inside this church before entering the confessional seemed to satisfy a deep need for meaning in my life as well, like the overt trappings of ritual with all those hundreds of candles flickering at all hours, the vaulted ceilings and the incense was just what was missing from my impoverished existence. I confess that I've led a life seriously in need of meaningful reflection. But for an instant once inside this church I felt a slight shiver that I suspect will always arrive unannounced into the bedrock of unshriven souls who may find themselves – for whatever reason – considering the end of life. I instinctively pulled back on the reins of my thinking, turning for a few moments toward thoughts of a pathetic life shaped mostly by avarice or sloth or pride rather than more virtuous qualities – and again shook off those thoughts by forcing myself to imagine an impossibly handsome, athletically oriented thirty-something priest who'd hear my confession. And he would be questioning himself too – his faith. And here I'd be, appearing in this confessional as if by magic – to smooth his transition from ignorance of the flesh to ultimate and abandoned knowledge – the satisfying element of his ecstatic curiosity. My presence would amount to a providential answer to his prayers; and his mine. So I was happy to make this little cubical my home for the moment, even though it was pretty clear after I'd awakened in the morning – and having been illuminated with the shrill light of sobriety – that the only thing missing from my life at that moment was cab fare.

So I won't judge Jimmy because I've been there. Jimmy doesn't seem to have outgrown this facet of meth fueled sex questing, though, and unfortunately for him he's become known to most law enforcement in quite a few areas of the city as somebody who creeps around private property trying to peek into windows looking for the perfect orgy. You get the feeling that the most interesting thing Jimmy's done in his whole life is watching game shows on TV, that and committing some really basic, unimaginative crimes like stealing bikes off the street or shoplifting stuff from Macy's. I don't think he's ever even forged a prescription. But again, he still looks pretty good from a distance.

It must be an unwritten rule: battles with gravity will inevitably push you farther and farther eastward. Los Angeles realtors know the value of youth, their mantra being: The Wester the Better – unless of course you might be, due to some kind of overt protest against the tyranny of valuation, lured in the opposite direction all the way down to Santa Fe and St. Julian where Skid Row is, where dick is cheap and plentiful. It's because of crack. Crack just makes shit weird, and the common denominator down on Skid Row is crack – I mean, besides that whole poverty thing, which probably has a lot to do with everything. It's probably a combination, the stupidity of crack and all that poverty. I've been down there a few times when I couldn't find any crystal, and you kind of need to have a guide with you who knows some local people because it's different down there. Things are flattened out. Definitions are basic, like you get the feeling that people who live on Skid Row will place your fucked up old pickup truck into the same category as a Rolls Royce. *Four-Wheel Vehicle = Four-Wheel Vehicle. Period.* There's almost a kind of elegance in its simplicity – almost. In West Hollywood or Silver Lake when you meet somebody you want to have sex with, there's like this awkward little confession time when you have to say whether you have HIV or not. But down on Skid Row, you try to be responsible and good citizens and divulge your HIV status, they just look at you weird, not because they're turned off or anything, it's like they just don't want to hear it. Period. They don't say anything, but you get the feeling they're thinking: *Jesus! What the fuck! Why did you have to complicate things any more than they already are?* Like they'll insist on sucking your dick anyway, but there's an added level of complication there that you get the feeling they'd just as soon not know about, and they pretend that they didn't hear what you just said.

The few times I got high on crack, I was lucky it didn't do anything for me. Just made me stupid. One time I drove my truck into a gas station and I got out and it was like I completely forgot what you're supposed to do at a gas station. I walked around my truck in circles like a moron trying to remember why I was there, but the crack made me too stupid to even be frustrated. I finally remembered that I was supposed to pay money and get gasoline but it took a minute. I didn't get all self-conscious and freaked out – I thought it was funny, even though I felt like when people looked at me they saw like a Picasso painting with eyes bunched up over on one side of my face and my mouth all crooked and bloated somewhere on my neck. And I guess I'm lucky though that I didn't go inside the little minimart and see if they got the joke too, like "Man, I got stuck on stupid for minute – get it?"

Another thing about Skid Row, the air's always smoky down there – and you kind of suspect that even smoking crack out in the air wouldn't create clouds of smoke like there is down there, and it smells like fireworks, but one thing for sure: no crackhead is gonna light firecrackers or cherry bombs or anything – that would be hilarious, come to think of it. Even if they had anything to celebrate down there, they're not going to light off fireworks because that would ruin the evenness of their little high – like it's a really strange version of that saying that used to be on a bank building in Hollywood that's from Lao Tzu: *The Even Tenor of a Well-Run State,* and it *is* kind of a state down there but the kind of state where all the citizens spend their waking hours quietly and earnestly looking for pebbles or pieces of drywall on the sidewalk or in the gutter or in the pile of the carpet because it might be unharvested pieces of crack that providence has overlooked, or walking around with these crazy-looking wild eyes, like they just shot their best friend in the face because they stole a piece of Chore Boy steel wool from them or stepped on their pookie or some equally serious transgression. Crackheads are like manatees, but really dimwitted and really slow manatees. Even if they're incredibly hot handsome guys with muscles and big dicks and they probably had girlfriends or wives in their pre-crack lives, crackheads will suck your dick and will totally be your lover even if they never thought about fucking around with a guy before if you can make them think you're their ticket to a few more pieces of crack.

I leave Jimmy S. to flop around in his stupor and I finally make it back to Korn's back room where the action is.

Billy B. consoles Sanchez who's been crying in the bathroom – he cries a lot, but there's no judgment here. Everybody has issues. Billy's trying to get Sanchez to finally accept the reality that RoyBoy isn't getting out of jail any time soon – his bail is over $100,000, even though nobody except Billy thinks that's why Sanchez is crying. He just cries a lot – I think he wakes up crying, which creates a kind of low-grade curiosity as to why he cries – although nobody really wants to go to the trouble of investigating the reason though – kind of like being mildly interested in a novel but because actually reading it would be kind of a chore, all you do is speculate on what it's about, using only the title or the cover art as clues for discerning its "aboutness." So without inquiry, any opinions about the cause of Sanchez's weeping would be as accurate as saying *Moby Dick*, by virtue of its cover art, its title and its mythos, is about a search for a giant white whale or about hubris or revenge – all three of which, while technically not incorrect, come as close to the truth about the novel's essence as claiming that capitalism, if left to grow on its own without any meddling from legislators, will sometimes sprout tiny delicate buds of altruism instead of its normal meat-eating blossoms that blot out most of the sunrise because they never sleep because they're always eating, eating, eating – devouring everything in sight, even the stuff that's probably not good for them, they're so damned hungry. A couple of guys have posited that Sanchez (who three weeks ago spent a meaningful nine-hour stretch at the baths with RoyBoy) cries because he realizes that if RoyBoy is seen outside the confines of the county jail anytime within the next six months, it's because he's probably given one or more of us up to the cops, so his freedom won't bode well for anybody and Sanchez may not want to accept the fact that Royboy has feet of clay, at least as it relates to his standing as a dope fiend. Poor Sanchez. Nobody's got honor these days. Everybody's a snitch and a snake. They'll all steal your dope and then help you look for it, and everybody will give you up if it'll keep them out of jail. But Sanchez's crying probably has nothing to do with Royboy – or anybody else for that matter. He probably just wants to get high. I mean everybody's kind of sad right now because nobody really knows how to act when there's no dope around, but this sadness usually manifests in maybe taking out the trash or heading over the needle exchange or doing other necessary, mundane stuff. Not one of us, though, even considers for even a tiny sliver of a moment that he might be crying because he's ashamed of what's become of his life – either that or the opposite, that he's begun to see exactly how weird it is to live life as a human being on planet Earth, especially if you insist on being fucked up all the time.

Sanchez looks at me with these sad red puppy eyes, and with a voice that's wobbling and cracking like it's suffering from timbre failure he asks me if I have any shit, "shit" meaning crystal meth, to which I answer in the negative. "Sorry," I say, then add that I've got a ton of Wellbutrins, which is a low-grade psych med that guards against depression and is a drug that the AIDS medical community views as necessary as air itself and that guys locked up in the gay section of county jail, in an attempt to at least pretend they're getting high, smash up and snort together. The jail cops started doling out Wellbutrins to prisoners right after the state made it illegal to smoke cigarettes in jail because it's supposed to smooth the transition into becoming a non-smoker, and transitions that are smooth instead of rocky, I guess the thinking was, makes for more peace between prisoners. Snorting Wellies objectively gives you less of a rush than maybe closing your eyes and running around in circles, but try to do that in jail – even one of the gay tanks where almost all the legitimate fags have AIDS – "legitimate fags" meaning that there's a large percentage of straight guys who've made it to Treasure Island because they know it's easier to do time in a gay tank than in the general population, and they know enough about fag life that they pass the sheriff's totally lame Gay Quiz with ease, which is like the equivalent of a gay GED test. These idiot sheriff's deputies – all of them that are assigned to administering this Gay Test – are rookies. They'll ask you questions like: "What's Micky's?" "Are you a top or a bottom?" the answers to which are "gay bar" and "bottom" because what else could Micky's be, and if you say you're a top, these young deputies, having the imaginations of cantaloupes, assume you're straight because of their belief that no straight guy, convict or not, would admit to getting penetrated, anally speaking – especially on the record, especially if it wasn't true. And criminals, straight or not, being their own unfiltered charming selves, like it's no skin off their asses, will swallow their pride and admit to climbing the dick tree every time if it'll keep them out of general population. If the cops were even a tiny bit more cunning about this test they'd ask a couple of questions about AIDS medication: "What regimen are you on?" "Do you take it on a full stomach or empty?" But they don't. They're not cunning. They avoid any questions about AIDS because they're probably afraid that it might be understood as some artifact – some palimpsest of compassion from some earlier millennium and there must be no doubt in anyone's mind that this jail facility has just about zero tolerance for anything resembling compassion, especially for guys of the homosexual variety. Running around in circles even in a gay tank would still be considered totally uncool.

My offer to share my bounty of Wellbutrins snaps Sanchez out of his pity party and, like he's at the leading edge of an extremely effete, super fatigued low tide of ill will, lashes out at me but it's hard to identify whether he's lashing out with that kind of sleepy slow-motion meth-freak hatred that struggles to roil just under the surface of the sleep deprived consciousness or just plain old garden variety ennui. Bringing up the rear of several sighs are the slurred words: *"What the fuck! What the fuck do you think this is? The fucking Thunder Dome? What the fuck am I gonna do with fucking Wellies…"*

And then, just like somebody flipped a switch somewhere, Sanchez hiccups quietly and announces in the friendliest of tones that he's going to take a nap. And this announcement is delivered in a way that's like zipping up your windbreaker in one seamless motion: zzzzip – silence – end of conversation. He heads off to a couch in an adjacent room, and just as he does the doorbell chimes followed closely by Korn's phone ringing. "Fuck" Korn hisses. As he reaches for the phone, he faces me with arched eyebrows and makes a turning door knob motion with his right hand silently asking me to see who's at the door. He doesn't say the words, but everybody knows what he means: *This traffic is gonna get us busted.*

A little while later we're sitting around a coffee table that's really just a giant kidney-shaped mirror with spindly black legs. It's cluttered with overflowing ashtrays, opened packs of cigarettes, and those long pastel-colored plastic straw-spoons they give you when you buy 7-Eleven Slurpies. Javier, who just arrived, shares with Korn, me and Kirkuleaz – and anybody else who wants to listen, that he's just left the local Neighborhood Watch meeting over at McKinley High School in the cafeteria there. Javier's an interesting guy. He stopped using drugs about nine months ago – he goes to NA meetings and he's totally sober all the time for several months now. But for some reason he feels totally connected to Korn, like he can't bring himself to pry himself away from Korn's house, so he still shows up here every day. He says that this Neighborhood Watch meeting was packed, and he hung out in the back because he didn't want to be ID'd as somebody who had a connection to this place because let's face it: Javier isn't the most masculine Latino aspiring drag queen in the world. That, combined with the fact that he could never be mistaken for being attached in any way to Korn's Jewish neighbors – except as maybe Esther Shapiro's ballroom dance instructor.

Three or four detectives from the LAPD were there in the auditorium giving kind of a presentation about keeping bad elements out of respectable neighborhoods like this one. And Korn is paying pretty close attention because he totally owns this house, and he especially listens close when Javier's voice gets a little bit quieter and he says that the main subject that the crowd wanted to talk about was Korn's house. And to underscore this point he takes a piece of paper he's got folded up in his back pocket, unfolds it and reads from it – it's the meeting's agenda. On top of the paper there's the seal of Los Angeles, but it's in Xeroxed black-and-white instead of the really colorful real one with the stars and stripes and the red rampant lion, the golden eagle and the brown bear, but still it looks kind of official. And there's several entries that mention the height of people's hedges and stuff and how Home Depot sells automatic light dimmers for not much money, and these dimmers will fool would-be crooks into thinking somebody's inside the house when they're really over at Norms eating dinner, or over at the temple, which will cause the thieves to stay away. But Number Three on this agenda – with no context or preamble or anything – is the address of Korn's house – just the street address, 2045 South Kenmore Avenue – this house right here. And with just the mention of this address at this Neighborhood

Watch meeting, which everybody there knows by heart, the whole auditorium kind of erupts into rowdiness, with people demanding when the LAPD was going to do something about "those dope addicts" who live here. And the people who were the loudest were the ones with the religious-looking stuff, like Jewish prayer shawls and long side locks. Javier says that an older guy with a beard and wearing a black hat started screaming that he's certain that we're here in their neighborhood because we are God's punishment for some sin they've committed. And these detectives, trying to be respectful but still wanting this guy to shut up, they just smiled and nodded, confessing that they didn't really know too much about God's plan to punish the people on Kenmore Avenue, but that they understood the man's concerns. A couple of the other men in the audience then tried to calm this guy down, and he stayed quiet for a while until he'd had a minute to think about the situation again. And once more he stands and tries to sound rational at first, keeping his voice on an even keel and kind of quiet, but it starts to crescendo and ejaculates into blisters and pustules of hatred, like he just can't help it. He's comparing Korn's arrival into their neighborhood with all the historical instances where Jews had been persecuted and he's screaming that Korn was *exactly* like the Christian cross that's planted in the open field that's right outside Auschwitz concentration camp; that the Gentiles have always hated the Jews and this proves it; that the cross there was just a symptom of a greater form of hatred that's always existed; that he understood completely that the Catholics lost a few hundred people at Auschwitz, and then he got quiet for a minute – "*a few hundred*" he repeated quietly a couple of times, and then he starts repeating the same thing each time getting louder: "A few hundred. A few hundred... *a few hundred Catholics and a handful of Carmelite nuns compared to the hundreds of thousands of Jews who'd burned at the hands of the Nazis at Auschwitz.* We" – and he gestures around to everybody in the auditorium – "are the *Temple,*" he says, "and – these drug addicts – these *hippies* – these *filthy diseased fagelas,* who're all free and breezy and do as they like, they're here to tear it down."

But he's not done yet. He says that even the goddamned cross itself was usurped by the Gentiles; that making the sign of the cross was first a Jewish thing, that Jews were doing this for hundreds of years before Christianity because they were, with this making-the-cross gesture, simulating the Hebrew letter that the word 'Torah' begins with and the goddamned Gentiles couldn't even let them have that. Then he says that it's obvious to him that the Gentile dope addicts were here to "supersede" all the Jews; and that it just starts with one person and then another and then more and more and then you have the Holocaust all over again. And this guy is starting to foam at the mouth and it's catching and various people around the room are screaming "Never again!" And the detectives had to calm the crowd down several times, all the while reassuring everybody there that they were aware of the situation and for everybody to try to be patient.

Korn's jaw just kind of goes slack, and he looks down. "Wow" he says. Then I guess to diffuse the tension he asks me if I want to run down to Antonio's with him and get a couple of burritos.

"Sure" I say, and we both head out the door, and just before the door closes behind us, Jimmy S. comes running up and he's asking where we're headed and he's all out of breath and it's obvious he's risen from his prolonged period of spaz hibernation. His red pompadour has been deflated and it's pretty clear that he probably hasn't even used the bathroom yet. I tell him we're gonna get some burritos and would he like to come with us. And he just looks at us weird like we're completely crazy and says "No, not hungry;" that he's just gonna head out for a while. I'm relieved he's not coming, and I say "Cool, be safe."

Antonio's is only a few blocks away down on Vermont – and it's open 24/7. We leave Korn's car in the driveway and head down Kenmore on foot. Neither of us says much though so we just walk, only occasionally mentioning dope craft and its attendant cast of characters and their dramas *du jour*. We both kind of notice a couple of guys who've been walking toward us at a right angle – actually I notice that they've noticed us – no big deal – just the usual Gaydar kind of thing. Between both Korn and me we concede to these guys at the appropriate moment a voiceless head nod, the subtext of which is the widely accepted "Wazzup?" meaning we're aware of them and further communication might be forthcoming. They nod back, offering their own silent "Wazzups" as we meet each other. We stop momentarily, turning our attention to them – for confirmation's sake: There's definitely interest there. We're definitely hovering, weighing our schedules and responsibilities against a possible sexual liaison which, admittedly, would be a nice distraction though, so Korn and I stupidly kind of just stand there gawking at these two guys. After a few really awkward moments, introductions are made: Hi, I'm so-and-so/Hi, I'm so-and-so, and so on. A few more moments pass in silence and the two kind of pull away from us – we're walking in the same direction now. We stop to watch these two guys receding from our view, but that's as far as it goes. The wisdom of pursuing such a seemingly huge diversion at the moment is questionable because the heaviness of Javier's' revelation re: the Neighborhood Watch meeting seems to want to us to focus on more serious stuff, and they're moving considerably faster than Korn and me. There's an occasional turn of the head along with additional slight nods between us and these other guys, but mostly Korn and I just walk in silence since almost all conversation at this point seems portentous, even though we're both buoyed somewhat by the fact that all four of us seem to be headed in the direction of Antonio's.

I think about God and about being inside Korn's house, and I can see it surrounded by all these people who hate us – well, maybe they don't really "hate" us because that would mean that they had some bit of behavior-centered context to base their feelings on – but they at least think we're evil. I think about the moms and dads and their kids and the whole thought of this question that they want answered more than anything: why are they being punished with our presence? And I think about *my* mom and dad and how different my upbringing must have been – we were low-grade Methodists – nothing, absolutely nothing rose to the level of existential punishment in my entire life. God was a guy with a long beard who lived in the sky and he had blue robes and thick white hair and he exerted less influence on us than the Ford parked in the driveway. I know his robes were blue because I won a Bible once that had colored pictures of God and Jesus and everybody. In order to win this Bible I had to recite the Ten Commandments to our church's entire congregation one Sunday morning, but I choked and only made it up to maybe Commandment Three or Four – but the pastor gave me the Bible anyway and everybody applauded my pathetic performance. My dad was bald and in our domestic life at home, my mom played the piano and danced all at the same time. They drank a lot and seemed to have a pretty good time. The whole idea of existence was never brought up, much less God's punishment for just breathing.

Even though Javier's description of the Neighborhood Watch meeting was pretty intense, this little walk to Antonio's seems to banish this harshness further and further away into some benign mental territory, and for some reason I get this vivid memory of John and Marsha from when I was like five years old and we lived in National City, which is a suburb outside of San Diego, and I know now that it's the closest thing to a ghetto I ever lived in, at least before I was an adult. John and Marsha were these two wasps that I claimed as pets – their home was inside a cardboard box that at one time held some large appliance like a stove or refrigerator or something. I just assumed they were married because there were only two of them, and there was this honeycomb-like stuff that was kind of silky – and I guess that's where I imagined they slept at night. Come to think about it though, I'm not even sure if John and Marsha were different genders or even alive or whether they were wasp corpses that I played with inside this cardboard box. I use the term "played with" kind of generously because all I really remember about my interaction with them was that Marsha would swoon in her soprano wasp voice when she said with great passion, John's name: *Oh, John!* And John being the male would then repeat Marsha's name when it was his turn, but in a resonant baritone – at least as much of a baritone as a five-year-old can muster: *Oh, Marsha!* And they'd continue on like that: *Oh, John! Oh, Marsha! Oh, John! Oh, Marsha!*

I ask Korn, who's walking beside me, if he ever had any pets when he was a kid, to which he says "Yeah, a medium-sized poodle named Bandito," end of comment. I want to share my memory about my pet wasps with him but I keep my mouth shut because – I don't know why, but probably because I don't know Korn very well and I'm afraid he'll maybe think I'm weird, meaning that I've misconstrued the nature of his invitation to Antonio's – that maybe I've elevated it to the level of sleepover, the kind when you were a kid and you tossed out avalanches of confession-tainted words detailing the facets of your pre-pubescent existence to every pajama-clad torso that was attached to heads with faces covered with microscopic pores and well-scrubbed sets of aural canals, the meaning of which might be understood as tiny proclamations of camaraderie and undying loyalty that are usually reserved for that variety of friend that exists in the realm of "best" – but most of all, I'm not exactly a hundred percent sure that this walk to Antonio's isn't a kind of a first date, and I kind of instinctively suspect that "confession" and "first date" can't exist together at the same time and place – except of course if, by some really cool existential somersault, the temperature in this part of Los Angeles has fallen to just above absolute zero, which would blow apart not only the binaries of confession/first date, but each and every one of them beginning with life/death; black/white and so on, and would render the whole concept of "burrito" or "date" moot and would actually kill not only our appetites, but both Korn and me too. I mean, I haven't dated anybody for years where you don't use drugs and the two of you go out and do something, like watch a movie. And neither of us is high, so I don't say anything because the last time I tried going on a date with somebody while we were both "sober" it was a disaster.

There was this weekend and I'd just moved into my place in Highland Park. And I had plenty of drugs but I didn't know any people at all except in Hollywood, which was miles away. I don't know what got into my head. I don't know what made me – I can hardly breathe the word – "lonely." I guess I was questioning myself – my lifestyle for a minute – or I was thinking what dope fiends always think: imagining a life where you can use drugs and have a meaningful relationship all at the same time – having your cake and eating it too – like that might have been possible. But that's beside the point now because I went ahead and did it: I called somebody I used to get high with to go and see a movie. I can see the folly of it now, but at the time, all I could see was the inadequacy of a life shaped by dope deals and motel rooms and syringes and bags of meth and containers of Dilaudid. So when I learned that Kevin and Barry had broken up, I went ahead and started spending more and more time with Barry. And it's not like I didn't consider the plusses and minuses when choosing somebody to hang out with either. I felt a certain kinship with Barry – we enjoyed the same music, he was good looking, he shot enough dope to kill an elephant, and our names both started with "B": Barry and Bert. And he never seemed to get arrested either, which is a major plus in my book. I mean, who needed all that drama of being separated due to going to jail, especially if you both got arrested and were in adjacent tanks and the only time you could see each other was during church on Sundays? Some guys thrive on that kind of shit, but not me.

I imagined a perfect relationship growing between Barry and me where we rented movies and listened to music and fucked like monkeys, all, of course, while completely twisted from shooting dope. In my mind we had a happy life of selling dope and doing chores around the house, like washing dishes, mopping the floor and other concessions to domesticity. There were even times when my thoughts meandered across the boundary of drug use that didn't include shooting meth, but was limited to a happy existence of smoking marijuana and rationally abandoning harder drugs instead to a life shaped by endeavor, albeit of a really minor variety. I know guys who just smoke pot. I've actually lived with some of them. And I conjured a similar existence for myself where I'd wake up, drink a cup of coffee and smoke a joint then head (on foot) to a legitimate workspace that was close by where I'd build furniture with hammers and saws and screws and glue and the appropriate sized pieces of wood. It wouldn't be easy but it would be fulfilling and most of all, I'd be happy and satisfied with life. But even the second or third time I'd entertained this notion, I knew it was bullshit. I'd tried it before. And by "try" I didn't actually *try* this scheme – I only made it to the wood working section of Home Depot where I admired power tools and daydreamed of building a chair, something that – because of my 100 percent lack of expertise on the subject – and my insistence on consideration of chair-building as a muse – probably cost me more energy in imagining the process rather than actually learning how to do it, and wore me out sufficiently that I headed back to my home where I dove into the spoon more eagerly than usual.

The only minus to a life lived with Barry was that he quacked, which is actually one of his charms if you think about it. When Barry got loaded, which was all the time, instead of speaking in English he quacked like a duck. Some people thought this was really weird but I understood it. Barry seemed to know that language was meaningless, at least the torrent of dope-induced paranoid police schemes and gang plots that fall out of most people's mouths while they're loaded…so a stream of quacks was just as meaningful in the scheme of things. Barry's quacking was kind of like a cat purring: he wouldn't do it unless he felt completely safe and at ease. But miraculously Barry agreed to go to the movies with me – sober – at least *sans* meth.

So there we are at the Arclight in Hollywood – and we aren't that loaded. We smoked a little dope in the morning is all. And we're sitting in the theater and that dorky-looking guy is giving his little speech about "Welcome to the Arclight" blah, blah, and the movie's only been on for a few seconds and Barry nudges me. I look over and he pulls out a couple of syringes from his shirt pocket and says really soft "follow me." So we pad out of the theater then make our way into the men's room and go into a stall, which at the Arclight they're about the size of a small condominium – and we shoot up these sizeable doses of meth, which it turns out was kind of a mistake looking back on it in hindsight. Because when you shoot meth, right when it hits you, you basically turn into a walking hardon. So the men's room at the Arclight becomes our own personal little motel room. We sort of set up house there and we're just hanging out, and whenever a good-looking guy walks in Barry and I kind of go crazy on him – Barry quacking like a motherfucker with his dick in his hand and me walking in circles with my pants around my ankles and jacking off with my eyes all wide like saucers and everything. And this goes on for a while until these security guards finally come in and "escort" Barry and me out of the theater. So that was my big date.

Besides the food at Antonio's, which is widely accepted as "pretty good" and definitely authentic is the joint's music, which is never allowed to blast louder than maybe "4" or possibly "5" on the loudspeakers' volume rheostat. It's the oom-pah-pah style of Mexican music that's never questioned for some weird reason, even though it would be interesting to trace how the Lutheran and obviously Teutonic oom-pah-pah provenance of Oktoberfest drinking music, with its maniacal allegiance to not only the maintenance of a strict three-quarter meter, the 1-2-3 numerical embodiment of OOM-pah-pah, but also the starched creases and collars of oom-pah-pah blaring musicians that, no matter if it's twenty Fahrenheit degrees outside or 120 degrees, they maintain their crisp edges. It would be great to learn how this music somehow found its way from *the fatherland* into the decidedly more laid-back Catholic souls of tamale-laden Mexican musicians.

The middle-aged guy working behind the window at Antonio's is a little on the plump side and he wears a too-small T-shirt with the word WOOF emblazoned across what in more athletic men is the area of the chest identified as their pectoral muscles. He's what's known in the community as a bear, or in less generous terms, the kind of guy who's found a way to capitalize on his aversion to exercise along with his considerable appetite for pasta, cheese and peach cobbler. Some guys in the Bear community have developed a pretty underhanded strategy for getting naked with other guys who might be in better shape. Painfully aware that no matter how deep into the animal kingdom they've placed themselves, some bears have – in an effort to locate habitually ingesting too much cholesterol into a neutral realm – they've created Awareness Groups – groups whose advertised purpose was to "raise" awareness, which would smooth the way for those who'd suffered a stumble or two on their ascent into twenty-first century American acceptance – where nakedness is mandatory and handling someone else's cock has deftly been plucked from the realm of desire and plopped smack dab into one they've labeled as honor-driven: *Would you mind if I "honor" your body? Would you mind if I "honor" your cock?* He's a nice guy though – almost too nice. And while he probably understands that the WOOF written on his shirt is an interjection connoting animalistic hunger/desire, he probably isn't aware that it embodies a desperate hope for reciprocal proclamations of desire emanating from both the desiring and desired: I'm woofing at you and inviting you to please – *please* – woof back at me. But in the case of this guy, WOOF remains a flaccid entity whose objects are so widely dispersed throughout the universe, both seen and unseen, that the concept of objectification will never escape the realm of the theoretical. This WOOF may have begun its life as a raucous declaration of horny intentions, but has eroded into a sad plea for simple acknowledgement. He's solicitous to a fault and I suspect he's extremely lonely.

Korn tells him that he wants two machaca burritos – and then he turns to me and says, "What do you want Bert?" And I think this is the first time I've heard Korn actually say my name. Bert. He actually knows the signifier for me. I know right away that I shouldn't thank him for remembering my name. I think I can read minds sometimes. I think I know how I come off to people, especially people like Korn. I've never considered that Korn might actually think of me in any way that didn't involve me paying him a wad of cash for a baggie of dope. I'm the guy with the arm that's attached to the hand that pulls out a wallet that's got money in it; the polite guy that thanks him for the drugs and leaves; one of the guys you say *be safe* to. I hate decisions, especially when it's the kind of decision that will reveal my burrito preferences, or those idiotic questions your doctor asks you every couple of months: Do you want to continue on with the Atripla? You seem to be doing well on it. Any complaints? I mean, how the fuck should I know whether I should stay on this drug or not. I thought that was the job of the expert, you know, the doctor? Those are questions designed to absolve the questioner of any responsibility at all, like if the drug was making me grow gills or sprout horns or a tail, then the doctor, who fears the lawsuit more than anything else in creation, could say truthfully while shrugging his shoulders that I, his patient, reported that he was fine with the drug. I mean doctors and everybody else have taken this whole representative democracy thing as far as it ever should have gone – because leaving the choice of not only who should govern but how they should govern is foisted on those who are objectively less qualified to make these choices as is Korn's Bandito or maybe my own little winged although probably dead John and Marsha. If doctors just grew a pair and just straight up told you that you're going in the right direction, that would be better.

I've always thought Korn was cute and sexy and I'm a little bit giddy about him offering to buy me a couple of burritos. What if he actually "likes" me? And no sooner than finding myself conjuring scenes of a courtship tinged by puppy love that begin to roll through my brain, I realize that I'm beginning to entertain the inevitable thoughts of infidelity. I can just see him cheating on me – tenderly cooing to another guy, his words slightly misshapen as they make their way around the syringe lodged lightly between his teeth – *that's right "may-me" because 'b's are hard to say when there's some foreign object in the way* – at the same time he gently slaps his *nouveau* partner's arms trying to coax sleepy veins to life. But before this awful thought blooms into the looming expression of my displeasure at being cheated on, *That motherfucker!*, I slam down the brakes and try to stay in the Antonio's moment. I don't want to turn Korn off by what comes out of my mouth, like if I say that it's okay, that I just want a Coke – or a Diet Coke, it would kill me if Korn's eyes glazed over, like at my age I was still watching my figure – at what age do guys stop watching their figures, even gay guys? And if I say, "Just a couple of taquitos," Korn might construe that as wasting a generous offer of sustenance on a dish that's objectively only slightly less trashy than a flimsy white cardboard skiff-shaped container stuffed with nachos that are smothered in hot cheese whiz and those weird peppers; or is an overt attempt at humility, which is something that really turns me off when I come across it. It's one of my big peeves – not even a pet one, but a real straight-up feral peeve: people who actually say they try to be humble in their daily lives. It makes me want to shake them by their shoulders: Don't you know that humility is one of those things that *just isn't talked about;* like as soon as you even utter the word "humility," the whole concept of humility starts to disintegrate – and saying the word will probably start a dialogue about humility, and people in the conversation will start sharing their little anecdotes about how humble they've been in their lives. And this polite conversation will hurtle toward its ultimate ruin, on and on for a while until it turns into a straight-up bitch fest, the ethos of which is: I'm more humble than you are, motherfucker – and people will lean over and snidely whisper to their best friends sitting on either side of them: "Look who thinks he's nothing…"

CHAPTER EIGHT

I tell Korn that I'll have whatever he's having, so he tells the guy behind the window that he wants two more machaca burritos for me, and two Cokes, and pays for them. The guy gives Korn some change along with our drinks in red-and-white cardboard cups and a couple of straws, that we each force through the indentations on the plastic cup lids. All very civilized. And after about maybe six minutes, the guy's voice comes on the loud speakers, and you can hear him clear as daylight, "number forty-three," which Korn right away knows is us because we're the only people there. He gathers up the proffered two red baskets loosely woven with a surprisingly un-flimsy form of plastic spaghetti, and that are lined with kind of stiff waxy paper that hold our burritos, which are in turn rolled up in what has to be the most delicate aluminum foil in the universe and more of the wax paper.

Until now I've been the model of demureness and etiquette. But I jump into action and lend Korn a hand, hoping that I don't look like I'm trying to be chivalrous, even though I'm pretty aware that I have about zero ability to shape what Korn or anybody else for that matter thinks about me. So what if I look chivalrous? At least I'm not an overt asshole, right? I mean I could have just assumed that he was leaving all these decisions up to me, and I could have based all my choices on that little baseless notion, which actually has a greater asshole-ness quality than trying to be polite. And this moment of rumination creates a space that allows a moment of indecision to sprout and bloom: *Dine In or Out?* wordlessly signified with just Korn's and my own very slight quizzical looks as our collective attention is drawn to the five or six blue and white metal tables all shoved to the back of a flimsy-looking lean-to kind of shelter, which may or may not qualify for being officially out of doors, which would designate either a smokeless or smoking permitted area in which to sit.

The sidewalk running alongside Antonio's and also Vermont Avenue is just now beginning to become populated with the east side masses, along with many of the fatigued, yet overly steeled night students at Los Angeles City College, who will sit cross-legged on the cold hard linoleum outside their classrooms for hours, all the while holding *ad hoc* study groups that most of these adult academic hopefuls, who all seem to be pushing forty, pray will shed some light on the dreaded *run-and-rise* equations that they'll be examined on in their looming algebra class.

"Here's fine with me," I say, outlining with my eyes the interior of Antonio's dining area, hoping that this will be okay with Korn. But I have my reasons. First of all, I'm hungry. It's been a while since I've actually eaten anything more substantial than Wheat Chex and Gatorade, and I know that dragging these burritos back to Korn's house will probably mean offering to share them with others – "others" being a generous term that's a pretty neutral descriptor for normal people who have normal lives and normal appetites, not the bevy of Kenmore Avenue hyenas who've endured multiple days of self-induced starvation, which would change the word "share" into a much more robust verb like "relinquish."

I sit and Korn follows suit, seating himself across the table from me.

There's this little instant of hesitation that seems to have sprung from some miraculous store of human evolution – a moment that separates human beings from coyotes or some other group of savannah-dwelling scavengers. Korn looks at me. Right in the eyes. "You hungry?" he asks. "Yeah," I answer. "Pretty hungry."

CHAPTER NINE

A note about Cri-Life:

Cri-Life is a hulking battleship gray overly modern-looking building, meaning that its design incorporates a lot of stucco-covered angles, large reflective windows and glass blocks, although there's an explicit nod to the Italian Renaissance within some faux parquet elements in the front. It was bought and paid for by the father of one of its original addict clients. So grateful was he that his son no longer injected substances into his veins that he wrote a check to Cri-Life, Inc. for $12 million. Having existed for close to thirty-five years, Cri-Life is one of Southern California's two main recovery homes designed to address addiction, most notably that of the heroin variety – the other facility being Impact House in Pasadena, again a six-to-nine-month program – both necessarily catering to a mostly criminal class of addict – the kind steeped in both the shoot-em-up-stabbing-car-jacking-ATM-robbing-or-stealing-multiple-cartons-of-Marlboros-from-the-local-CVS-Pharmacy-then-fleeing-on-foot variety of crime and also the more dramatic suitable-for-a-major-motion-picture-starring-Bruce Willis-or-Brad Pitt-sawed-off-shotgun-wielding-major-narco-jacking-literally-barrels-of-cash-grabbing-then-buying-two-or-three-E-Class-Benzes-one-for-you-and-the-other-one-for-you-too-because-money kind of crime, both varieties of which render said principal addicts major criminals in the eyes of the Justice System, and when realized as components of a Venn Diagram exist in a hazily purplish shaded area of intersection, one side of which is a large blue partial circle labeled Recovery House with its focus on reintegration into society so therefore forward looking and very touchy/feely with a maximum of talking, listening, meditating and praying, pats on the back and weekend passes; and the other side a red partial circle labeled straight up Maximum Security Prison so-don't-worry-we've-got-automatic-locks-on-every-door-and-no-motherfucking-criminal-scumbag-type-of-client-can-even-think-of-doing-something-stupid-because-we've-got-him/her-under-a-level-of-scrutiny-that-would-embarrass-even-the-best-built-most-well-thought-out-panopticon-described-in-any-critical-theory-text-you-can-find-in-any-humanities-program-on-earth.

And this Recovery structure has been proven over and over to be more successful and more cost effective than simply locking someone up in prison, facts stressed with major repetition to most magistrates in most courtrooms not only in Southern California but more and more in all the other forty-nine states as well. (There is a third smaller circle of this Venn Diagram that intersects with the other two – one colored in a pale sky blue – just slightly more blue than white – which changes the shade where all three intersect only slightly because of its minor representation and is labeled simply "Other": those members of society whose transgressions were more moral than legal and reside in the realm of toast-burning-because-she's-twacked-housewife or pain-med-pilfering-nurse-on-a-burn-ward; "Other" also includes present-day victims of HIV/AIDS who've insisted on continuing to use drugs because they're rebelling against medical progress because they've grown totally comfortable with the notion of impending death and whose stays at Cri-Life are often funded through the Ryan White Act, Ryan White being the prepubescent, adorable yet most likely heterosexual kid who unfortunately succumbed to AIDS, which he caught due to sloppy and objectively non-gay transfusion practices because any overt governmental funding named after Trixie Boots, the aging cross-dresser, or The Rogarth Act or the Gallagher Act – taking for granted that in order to have one's name adorn any kind of governmental legislative maneuver they would usually need to stop being alive – in addition to the fact that each of said namesakes actually chose to suck dick so their names could never be considered even for a long list of candidates for whom to name a bill after because said names would need to be uttered in congressional budget hearings so do the math. So judges and DAs happily, at least for initial or even post initial but not overly recidivistic legal transgressions, with little regard to a crime's intrinsic seriousness, happily allow most who request it to be allowed to enter the doors of Cri-Life instead of moving directly to a jail cell. The really interesting byproduct of this judicial/administrative willingness to circumvent incarceration has imbued this locked-down style of recovery house with the same status of House of Worship – at least how said houses were once regarded in the Middle Ages: Once inside, the criminal is now known officially as "resident" and is therefore entitled to all perks and privileges afforded by the official doctrine of "sanctuary." Law enforcement officials, including Homicide Detectives, are denied access to all who've been assigned a pillow on which to lay their felonious heads once inside the legal king's X known as Cri-Life.

Week Two – Cri-Life, Inc.
Step Study – main dining room – 8:30 a.m. – every day except Sunday.
Mandatory attendance by all 130 residents in the facility.

The dining room is converted into a venue that ideally becomes an NA revival meeting where one of the twelve steps to recovery is read aloud and discussed, but that often veers pretty quickly to the path of least resistance, which usually means sharing with varying degrees of flair one's transgressions against society, which honestly is a lot more entertaining than trying to maintain interest in the landslide of stories focused on how abiding one's faith in god is. Depending on which CDW oversees these get-togethers, the step study is either a regimented parochial classroom run in a manner that's consistent with the tenets of the Dopamine Reduction Act of 1998 or kind of an after-breakfast-before-lunch dinner theater where the facilitator puts on a show that encourages attendees to discard their inhibitions and debilitating dope fiend pride that usually manifests itself as laser-focused awareness of even a morsel of perceived disrespect, which honestly must be some kind of relief because that kind of vigilance against something so common and so ridiculously subjective must be fucking exhausting, even though it's totally understandable if that's all you've got to be pissed off about, being disrespected, which is necessarily the case in most jail facilities.

It's these step studies where doubts about sobriety disappear, depending on who's running them. It's a time to stoke the fires of unbridled enthusiasm not only for a drug-free life that awaits after treatment ends, but also the two hours of obligatory daily cleaning of the facility that occurs directly after the obligatory prayer that marks the end of Step Study.

Today's focus, Step Five: Admitted to God, to ourselves and to another human being the exact nature of our wrongs.

Shoshanna B.: Length of stay at Cri-Life: Indefinite, but no less than one year.

Shoshanna's lengthy stay of time here is due to the fact that she enjoys robbing tanning salons in popular touristy parts of town. She is a drug addict. It's widely believed by the powers that be that Shoshanna avoided state prison due to her criminal-drug-addict-with-a-heart-of-gold-appearance/demeanor: She's an enormous white girl, about the size of a Volkswagen, with long, thick, unruly blonde hair framing an angelic yet seriously devious looking face with a pink, pinched mouth that's capable of releasing such a flood of explicit and truly nasty sexual as well as astoundingly violent ideas that you'd like to peel back her epidermis just to see whether or not there's actually a human being under there or some weird smorgasbord of electronics and animatronics that all work together to make up a vulgar robot girl that was designed to scare the kink right out of your Christian capillaries. Given the proper amount of distance and thoughtfulness about Shoshanna, though, it becomes probable that her potty mouth/potty brain, rather than being some ingrained predisposition, has been incubated as a result of her lack of male contact (Cri-Life has a policy called "Non-Com," which prohibits any interaction at all between the sexes, which, it's hoped will limit the number of Cri-Life fostered pregnancies to just under a "few" per year). The Non-Com umbrella is comprehensive and fluid and includes any and all direct communication between the sexes, but may, and usually does include a scenario when a female client on one side of the room overhears and laughs at a joke told by a male client to one of his buddies on the other side of the room. Even though Non-Com was designed to obviate sexual contact between male and female clients at Cri-Life, the homos are necessarily exempt and can and must freely exchange ideas with the objects of their desires. This may seem like an unfair advantage, but the administrations got it covered in a policy labeled "over-association," which amounts to staff members notating and sharing hierarchically their opinions/observations that Linda P. follows Lydia T. around most of the time, or David O. and Oscar P. are inseparable, which creates an enhanced level of scrutiny that it's hoped will provide a barrier against same sex fellatio or cunnilingis or even some mild groping.

During the particular heist that brought Shoshanna to Cri-Life's front doors, after threatening the owners and employees of *Melrose Beach* with a gun, Shoshanna tied them up but then apologized profusely even offering to make phone calls to loved ones and then walking next door to Tammy Tang's, an overpriced Thai restaurant, and purchasing a plate of shrimp pik pau and cashew chicken from the To-Go menu so that her victims would have something to eat after defeating their restraints, even though Shoshanna could have saved a bit of cash by planning ahead and buying said dish ahead of time from Wokano on Hollywood Boulevard because dishes on Thai menus are for all intents and purposes pretty much standardized, rendering the only difference between the pad Thai bought between restaurants across town from each other merely the difference between $8 and $18.

Although Shoshanna has been sentenced to at least a year behind the Cri-Life walls, her attitude here is pretty much formed and bolstered on a daily basis by the fear of not appearing to the House staff as being sufficiently enthusiastic about her recovery, which translates into basically one thing: eagerly participating in every activity no matter how lame you really think the activity is, the first of which offered on any particular day is step study.

CDW Janice E.'s favored means of facilitation is herself. She's is a force of nature, and her step studies will melt even the most cynical hearts and souls and will move even the most ossified prison-baked hardened motherfuckers to abandon any previous overt coolness in favor of the promise of a new drug-free life shaped by the satisfaction of paying bills on time, keeping appointments and feeding the dog, much of which Janice accomplishes by contrasting her previous drugged life, which consisted a lot of the time of sucking cheesy cocks behind dumpsters that rest in scary alcoves around MacArthur Park for a morsel of crack or a taste of heroin, to her respectable, well-scrubbed middle-class existence post sobriety. This level of public confession with its plentitude of sordid details is common in NA and is designed to let most neophytes know that they're welcome no matter how far down the pit they've fallen. She describes the addict brain and its attendant poor decision-making properties as Radio K-Fuck: *You all know – you know about Radio K-Fuck. Should I knock that lame white motherfucker over the head and take his wallet and his car, or should I just move along?*

This rhetorical strategy – the *you all know I been places, seen things and done shit, so jump on the wagon with me because you got nothing to lose* – elicits a satisfying roar of approving guffaws from the crowd and paves the way for Janice to pull out her big guns: The Hokey Pokey. No shit. The get-into-a-big-circle-and-put-your-right-foot-in; put-your-right-foot-out...turn-yourself-around-and-do-the-Hokey-Pokey Hokey Pokey. The amazing thing is that it works. This whole room full of cooler-than-shit dope fiends and tattooed convicts get into it. They shake their outstretched feet and their bony asses and Hokey-Pokey their way to the happy realization that they too, at any given moment in the continuum of regular, meaning unimpaired time, can choose to stop being cool and just be lame as shit, like Janice knows that deep down inside dope fiends want the same stuff as everybody else so it's okay to admit that you have fantasies that involve a front yard with a picket fence and a dog and whatever. What's especially cool about Janice's use of the Hokey-Pokey is that it seems to be an overt middle-finger salute to the usual recovery house strategy that involves nailing down the "underlying causes" of addiction. It's like Janice can see that "underlying causes" amounts to an avoided-at-all-costs puddle of excrement that needs to be detoured around. She equates addicts opining about underlying causes as a recovery strategy out of addiction to people who spend all day every day hanging out at AA/NA clubhouses and dispensing advice about how to get a job rather than just going out and actually looking for one. She compares any New Age strategy for dealing with unwanted behavior, which usually consists of a five-minute recitation of various life-affirming aphorisms (usually into a mirror in the morning before breakfast), with diseased people who are stricken with infection after infection, and who, in an effort to address their conditions, have forgotten that they've set up house in a lake of raw sewage. Even the hardened nihilism of many of the gay AIDS-stricken residents' melts away. But honestly it's probably not because they're jumping on the Life! bandwagon because Janice E's Hokey-Pokey has enabled them to envision a future that's shaped by being funneled into the ranks of tax-paying, cruise-taking, mortgage paying, flag saluting members of society, nor is it the result of not wanting to be perceived as a stick in the mud by any of the impossibly handsome prison transplants who are making an honest effort, it's probably because they simply like to dance. Regardless of motivations, it's a miraculous experience that truly lifts spirits into states greater than themselves. The downside of this experience is that there's only one Janice E. in the whole facility, and the running of step study is spread out among all the other CDWs, most of whom are morons like Rick with the teeth and the useless law degree and the royalty-rubbing social climbing parents. The step studies realized by most of these minor CDWs run the gamut of uncomfortable platitudes whispered by painfully self-conscious guys in their thirties who pace the room while looking at their shoes for the whole hour, to grinning human cornucopias brimming with sunshine (*turn that frown upside down*) and happiness, to bitter Gestapo barking false teeth clattering, respect demanding authoritarians who run the step study like classrooms where laughter is forbidden because being clean and off drugs is serious motherfucking business and you could die if you go back out there and start using again.

Janice's Hokey-Pokey has worked its magic. Gangsters begin allowing their dork flags to fly – even Rogarth's carefully woven shroud of self-conscious faux complexity has begun to unravel and he's actually surprised himself by shouting: "*...that's what it's all about!*" after about ten minutes of group dancing and shaking his ass. He doesn't want it to end but end it must. With a look from Janice everybody quickly and quietly sits.

Shoshanna pounces on her opportunity and volunteers to read

before anybody else, even Rogarth, who's sitting directly across from her, and who has, like a prepubescent periscope timidly peeking through an expanse of unfriendly ocean teeming with enemy battleships, inched his right hand up to volunteer to read as well, a gesture not unnoticed by Janice, who's got an abiding sense of fairness and is a champion of the underdog, especially gay underdogs, because Janice E. is a lesbian who now and then prefers her people and will often bestow favor on the homosexual rather than any number of heterosexual volunteers. With Janice E.'s blessing Rogarth usurps Shoshanna's place in the reading order and reads the step, after which, just like he's a total expert at this recovery thing, he releases a gusher of gratitude, thanking Cri-Life and Janice E., his buddy Gallagher, and the entire staff of Cri-Life for finally giving him this opportunity to finally grow up and be a man; that he's aware that it was anybody's guess how long it would have taken for him to shoot enough crap into his veins to kill him; that he's pretty sure he knows his drug use is due to unacknowledged terror at having been infected with HIV for decades, and he describes in detail a litany of awful things he's done to other people over the years, some of which aren't even true, but he's on a roll and why the hell not. And it's not as if the details tumbling off Rogarth's tongue at the moment have remained unedited.

There are certain facets of his life that he instinctively knows will prove unhelpful in any sense if uttered out loud in public or even private forums. A memory of his PCP-using years bubbles to the surface where he and his partner in crime – an elegant queen named John Royce – had both contracted hepatitis (the kind from dirty needles). And during the course of this sickness they'd each also picked up a virulent case of crabs. And during one quiet night of drug-induced unconsciousness and obstinate scratching, almost serendipitously, they both decided to infect hepatitis-free people they didn't like by picking the crabs off their pubic areas and dropping them into a tiny glass jar where they would be stored until such time as they might be collected and tossed onto the objects of their enmity. Of course this never came to pass for any number of reasons, the main one being the half-life of a drug addict's ability to remember stuff – that and the fact that keeping crabs alive inside a glass jar was about as workable as trying to transport fireflies from the Midwest to California inside glass jars. They always died at just about the Oklahoma border. And as Rogarth's in the middle of this confession (sans crabs and liver disease, of course) his voice cracks and he sobs a little bit and the whole room erupts into this supernova of appreciation for his honesty, something that Rogarth quickly and pretty much automatically perceives as the tiniest chink in the impregnability of the wall of twelve-step modeled recovery because he senses that the crowd's characterization of his confession as "honest" is completely based on context rather than even one morsel of essential content. Because he's admitted and given voice to details appearing to the closed set of Stephen Spielberg characters – or recovery house residents – or what's generously described too often as "the American public" to be somewhat raw and therefore private, they've been bestowed with the quality of "honest," a weakness of perception that Rogarth banishes to an "unimportant" part of his consciousness because he can see little use for it at the moment, as any personal benefit to be gained by using this insight as leverage resides beyond his perceived horizons, except maybe, in some remotely future desperate financial predicament where he might finagle his way up through the ranks of twelve-step service to finally earn the title of treasurer for this or that meeting which would burden him with the substantial responsibility of being the trusted collector of the approximately twenty-seven dollars in weekly donations added to the robust sum of $127 as a prudent reserve, a title suggesting that even after the imminent and dreaded yet amazingly completely unplanned for 7.0 earthquake predicted to destroy Los Angeles, The Architects of Adversity 12:30 p.m. Tuesday meeting that's held in the Senior Recreation Room at San Vicente Park would still be able to provide cookies and coffee to its sober members for five or six weeks without losing a beat even while the rest of the city smolders in ruin. He restrains himself from voicing his concerns: *Rather than thanking me for my honesty you should be thanking me for "sounding" honest, because you don't have any idea at all whether what I've said really happened or is complete bullshit.* Regardless, Rogarth's performance has set the tone for the remainder of Step Study and everyone who shares for the rest of the hour reveals facet after facet of shame and regret for acts they've committed against mankind and society.

Janice E.'s been listening quietly, focusing almost all her attention on Rogarth, who she's aware has only been a resident here for a little over a week. The parable that best describes her Rogarthian thoughts at the moment is *The Tortoise and the Hare*, the tortoise being the creature who's most likely to internalize the life lessons afforded by Cri-Life. Janice E. makes a mental note to keep an eye on Rogarth, the Hare.

CHAPTER TEN

I want to eat the fucking burritos but something's restraining me. I look at them both all nestled inside their wax paper and foil nest. Steam rises from the beans and rice and the red sauce. I don't look up but I know Korn's studying me, which almost makes my appetite for food dry right up. "Cheer up," he says as he takes a sip of his Coke – "Becky Stein's gonna drop by the house in a couple of hours." And this announcement makes me feel like I've just swallowed a couple of bowling balls. I've heard about Becky Stein for years but only met him once. He sells meth – large quantities of meth. But more than that, people say he's killed people before – with a gun. He's kind of like the gay *Kaiser Soze*, meaning that almost 100 percent of what's known about him is from stories people tell – whispered stories of ruthlessness and danger and serious dope deals.

The one time I met Becky Stein was a couple of months after I'd moved into my tiny bungalow in Highland Park. By some weird inversion of fate I seemed to be one of the few guys in Los Angeles during this one weekend that had any meth at all, which is doubly weird because I'd just started selling the shit. I spent an inordinate amount of time memorizing (*sans* flash cards) the various denominations and their attendant nomenclatures and weights: eight-ball = one eighth of an ounce; teenager = one sixteenth of an ounce (this designation is a pretty accurate measure of the limits of the meth freak's imagination, which is disappointing and reassuring all at the same time); gram = one gram (duh); quarter = a quarter gram (don't sell these – they're more trouble than they're worth, having the ability to lure the most people with the least money to your front door and will pretty much guarantee that pathetic petty criminals will be pounding at your door into the wee hours of the morning begging to be given one last dispensation), and which electronic scales were preferred and why.

I must say that it was a giddy feeling – when you're the only guy with any product – you all of a sudden become a total hot property and really really popular. Against what was usually understood to be prudent dope dealing practice I'd allowed anyone who wanted to, to come over and buy their meth – a strategy that often gets people busted if it continues on a regular basis.

I was blazing away higher than a motherfucker all weekend, slamming speed, smoking weed and fucking boys like I was a celebrity rock star. I'd received a call from a guy I kind of knew who said he wanted to bring Becky Stein over to get a couple of ounces of product. Allowing someone to introduce a stranger to buy drugs is just plain stupid and isn't done except under extraordinary circumstances, which usually means that the stranger has been described as an undiscovered porn star whose got an enormous cock that stays hard for hours – or that he's a celebrity of sorts, which Becky Stein certainly was. Everybody's heard about him. One thing I enjoy while I'm high on meth is to play the piano – I can play for ten hours straight – Mozart and Bach and Beethoven and a little Brahms when I feel capable. So I'm all alone in my little house at the moment and I'm waiting for this friend of mine to show up with Stein – and I confess that something I do is to try to impress people I don't know very well by letting them overhear me playing as they approach my front door. I wanted to make a real impression on Stein so I thought I'd mount an esoteric musical assault on him by playing Bartok as kind of an experiment, rather than the expected Beethoven or Brahms warhorses, just to see how this storied criminal would react to what's often perceived by naïve listeners as unwholesome music with all its incorrect-sounding modal melodies that can evoke to the uninitiated ear a pleasant unhurried stroll down paths inside a meat-packing plant while ankle-deep in rotting entrails; and clustered harmonies that look on the page like disparate groups of flies massing here and there on a piece of rotting fruit; and percussive, deceptively-simple-sounding rhythms – a process that's kind of like showing David Lynch's film *Blue Velvet* with its un-self-conscious yet brutal portrayal of Pussy Heaven with its kidnapped children jealously guarded by prim-looking widows tethered to their chairs by the awful weight of deadly secrets; and abandoned homosexual gangsters who lip-sync sad ballads to psychopathic sadists in order to earn a morsel of cock, for film aficionados who've only been exposed to movies like *The Little Mermaid* or anything with John Cussack. The piece I chose to let Becky Stein "overhear" was from Book Five of Bartok's *Microcosmos* titled "Boating" or "Kahnfahrte," the title of which has since been changed for some reason probably having to do with accuracy of translation to "Kahnpartie." I prefer "Kahnfahrte." Regardless, "Boating" is a lovely and tiny (two pages) piece of piano music designed for the pianist to gain facility in independent movement between the left and right hands. Grout's *History of Western Music* describes much of Bartok's music, at least in terms of its tonality, as being "on" a certain key rather than "in" a key. "Boating" seems to "on" the key of G major, as it ends with a wisp of a cadence like a G major feather that only reveals its tonality by lightly brushing the surface of a world where there's a shoreline that's only slightly G-ish. Bartok used the time signature of 3/4 in "Boating," meaning three quarter notes per measure. Simple. So I play. There's a motif that begins in the left hand that's evocative of movement *through water – a small boat cutting across the glasslike surface of a misty pond at dawn – experienced by only the person inside the boat.* I see above the staff a penciled-in single script letter "B" followed by lower case "e" and I have a vague recollection that once years ago I had started to write the word "Beautiful" there but thought better of it and stopped myself. Decades earlier, in an uncommon moment of un-self-consciousness, I'd actually written the word "beautiful" above a phrase of a Beethoven sonata I was playing. It was one of those unhurried, unadorned four-part chorale settings in C major that Beethoven was known to slip in between far-flung virtuoso sections in f minor or A flat or something – a peasant's prayer, a rare place of thankful respite – after a blinding tonal sojourn through the unknowable outer spheres of the universe where fear of the unknown is only mitigated by the steadiness of counting: four quarter notes per measure, 1 2 3 4, 1 2 3 4 – the reassuring tyranny of meter guiding the pianist, as he is able to literally see, through the veil of shifting tonalities into which admittance was granted, one after another, through the hidden portals of newly discovered pivot tones forming the corners of augmented sixth chords, Beethoven snatching the laurel crown from Napoleon's head, even his tacit approval for the newly minted French despot withering in the blink of an eye. What spirit! And I would have done the same thing – it couldn't have been any other way: great music would always outshine the pettiness of conquest. And it never should have ended. The simple act of writing above this stark white chorale the word "beautiful" with all its bald-faced subjectivity had carried with it an intensely personal meaning for me, like it was *my* version of a prayer, the embodiment of my respect for Beethoven, as I sat in the presence of greatness. I can see the folly of writing "beautiful" on anything now. It's a meaningless word.

So I'm playing "Boating" with its 3/4 meter and tonal center of G. I'm cutting through the water – it's nice – and I hear a stirring at my front door but no knock. Good. They're listening. Emboldened, I crescendo when the theme switches hands. Good. Back to the lonely boat at dawn. It's kind of poetic. There's a knock. I stop playing and answer the door. There's my friend – I think his name was William but it could have been Mike – and I quickly usher William or Mike and two other guys through the door, knowing that this gesture of speedy admittance will be appreciated by folks of the dope buying variety, as malingering on doorsteps as a prelude to purchasing drugs is totally frowned upon. They enter. William or Mike says this is Becky Stein and Kenyon something or other. Stein and this other guy only vaguely nod to me, giving almost all their attention to my piano which I must say is an impressive-looking black instrument: just shy of concert grand that takes up almost the whole room. Stein and his friend look more like college professors than gangsters.

"Bartok, huh?" Stein says.

I'm stunned, and without moving a muscle I reconstruct my previous conception of Becky Stein. My whole understanding of "gangster" and "scary" has been blown apart. What else might he know, I'm wondering. I imagine him commenting about my piano:

"I know why you're your piano is a Yamaha and not a Steinway."

I silently mouth the word "Why?" accompanied with arched eyebrows, tacitly encouraging Stein to please continue.

With a knowing sideways glance and a slight smirk, he says: "Because of the blood, silly!"

Stein keeps two steps ahead of me: "Don't be coy," he says in response to my look of befuddlement. "If this piano were a Steinway, you'd never have started selling drugs, you wouldn't have been jacked for your drug money, and you wouldn't have been stabbed last month – and there would be no blood – on this Yamaha thing. If this piano were a Steinway, it would go without saying that you'd know the plodding pain of sacrifice – you might be living here, but probably not. And you and I would probably never have met. Things would have turned out differently. You would have mourned the deaths of all those thousands of your brothers who succumbed to AIDS, because that's what you do when everybody around you dies, isn't it. But you didn't. You looked away – you got 'high,' because death is – what's a word you might use? Icky? Instead of bowing to the richness of the mourning process – the tragedy of prematurely dying – the inevitability of death – I hate to use the 'r' word because, in the scheme of things I don't really have much standing to use it, but what the fuck: the Responsibility. You insisted on superficiality. You could have stopped for a minute to consider the lay of the land – to maybe lend a hand to all those guys who died because treatment came too late – the ones with the lesions who got that 'look' that you get when you only have a couple of weeks left, or even to attend even one goddamned memorial for any of them who were your friends. Ok…you went to a couple of memorials, but you weren't present…you were fucked up. You weren't there to mourn, were you? You zeroed in on whoever was loaded there too. You acted like it was a fucking bath house, surreptitiously following guys into the bathroom where, after you had sex, you both traded nasty quips about the desperate cheapness of the memorial, saying stuff like, 'Do you believe those little cheese cubes on toothpicks?! My memorial's going to be held on the cliffs of the ocean and there will be a grand requiem playing really loudly and all the guests will wear white.' You went beyond merely cheapening their deaths. You ignored their deaths. Or that trip to France? Remember? You and that vulgar fat girl – Marsha – the one from Texas – and you just 'had' to see that Cathedral in Liege that was built using mortar made from the bones of thousands of French soldiers killed in World War I? Your behavior there would have mortified anybody with any sense. You ignored the tens of signs prominently remonstrating visitors to keep their mouths shut during their visits there. But you and your friend were drunk and nattered on like teenagers during lunch break. You insisted *on being as vulgar as you could, just like you did after 9/11, remember? Instead of sending heartfelt condolences – or just doing nothing at all – you know – being 'silent,' you got high, and in your insanity, you constructed overtly frivolous, impossibly silly-looking shaving caddies decorated with glitter, fake jewels and curlicues that you said you wanted to send to the survivors of the deceased first responders, you know, the firemen and policemen, those selfless brave men and women – imagining the stunned disbelief of the befuddled recipients of your work reading the included sentiment: 'Hi, I made this for you because I know you're probably really upset about losing your family 'n' friends 'n' stuff.' But you didn't, though, because that would have required you to actually dredge up enough courage to make yourself vulnerable for a couple of seconds. You kept your shaving caddies, prominently displaying them as totems to your irreverence. But your piano's not a Steinway, is it."*

I want more than anything to ask him how the fuck he knows all this shit – because I really *was* jacked a month ago – and stabbed. I'd say I was almost killed, but I'm not sure that's actually true because I don't really have a baseline to compare it to. All I really remember is at like four a.m. the electricity goes off which plunges the house into total darkness and makes the Bob Marley CD go silent. I went outside to investigate and was met by a surly looking guy who demanded to know if I was Bert. *"You Bert?"* he asked. My response was shaped completely with similar scenes I'd seen on TV and at the movies: *"Who wants to know?"*

Anyway, he pushes me up to my little front porch and I put on an anemic pantomime of resistance and was met with another person – a shadowy figure darting by who, in a split second, thrust a thin blade between a couple of my ribs – a quick in-n-out. That I was sure of – there's no doubt. *I've been stabbed.* Quickly and completely cowed, I ushered this big surly guy into the house and of course it's still totally dark because no electricity. He demands to know where the money and dope are all the while shoving me through the house and into the tiny bedroom, knocking over furniture along the way and me spilling blood all over everything including my piano. He tells me to kneel, which I do, and I'm actually pretty clear headed, which surprises me. *"Where's the money and dope,"* he again demands. I want to say something like: *You stupid motherfucker! If you hadn't cut off the electricity, I could get it for you.* But I think I just said that the dope and money are in the safe, which is across the room. He pulls out a gun – I didn't see it – but he pushes what I imagined was the barrel against the back of my head. *"Where's the fucking dope and money!? I'm gonna put a cap in your ass motherfucker!"* something that's never been said in my presence, but the words made me believe that it actually was a gun digging into my skull. My thoughts embodied my outrage. *This is* patently *unfair! He's already* stabbed *me, now he wants to* shoot *me!* where in my mind I'm standing, hands planted on hips, expressing my considerable indignation… Then, as if offering to the gods my sad opinions about the erosion of human values in this current day and age, all the while shaking my head in profound disappointment: *Where… is… his… sense… of… fair… play!?* as if like me his values had been shaped by the childhood experience of fucking up the Ten Commandments in front of his family's Methodist congregation. But instead I start sobbing and say these snot-tinged words: "I don't know where anything is…I can't see…it's too dark." I can feel blood oozing down my torso and moistening my clothes, and it's becoming hard to breathe, which makes me think that my lung has been pierced. I fish my wallet out of my pants and give him what's inside, about $600. He left before the dope was found. *I was jacked and I was stabbed.* But I lived, which is probably due to the ambulance that arrived after I'd begged – no shit – I had to fucking beg the managers of the little courtyard of tiny bungalows – which, when viewed through squinty eyes, any newcomer there would have said it loosely resembled a kind of utopia, mainly because it was miniature and well-kept and kind of a progressive island in the middle of an ocean of Hispanic superstition that made up Highland Park's gun/gang laden population. There was a center lawn and a few trees and shit – it was pretty fucking precious – and the managers reluctantly condescended to call 9-1-1 on my behalf even though I couldn't have made it clearer that I was probably dying – because they've lived in Highland Park long enough that their reaction to violence had evolved into a survival-heavy doctrine of non-intervention: *I see nothing; I hear nothing.* But they must have called because an ambulance finally showed up just as the sun was rising.

It was, I'll always remember, quite a beautiful sunrise, all a sleepy deep orange tinged with spots of bright yellow and deep purple, the purple being the result of the remnants of smog that still haunted LA's skies. And the coolest thing about ambulance people – the EMTs – is how you're made to feel like a commodity with no name – you're just some guy that's probably dying, but they're so fucking efficient that all you really feel is gratitude. I'm loaded into this big clean ambulance and there's two uniformed females and one impossibly handsome guy who immediately scans my arms looking for a place to start a line. As if I'm not even there he says, "*Jesus! He's* (meaning me) *totally torn up*" – not referring to my stab wound, but the state of my arms. I'm what's known as a "hard stick," meaning that my veins are shot. His proclamation is tinged with disgust, which makes me feel like – um – shit, and I look to one of the females and say, "*Who the fuck is this guy?*" And this female EMT looks down and puts a finger over my mouth: "*Shhhh – he's saving your life.*" And I didn't feel fear or much of anything except regret at that moment – I guess that even for proud dope fiends, circumstances sometimes will pull everything into perfect focus. The context of me was finally – *finally* in its correct position. *I don't want to die like this. Dying like this is just so vulgar – tedious almost – cheap.* But my very next thought was that getting shot with an inexpensive pistol was probably a little bit more common than being stabbed like this in the scheme of things, which didn't make me feel much better but I suppose you grab what you can.

I pry myself away from these thoughts – it can't continue because I'm almost a hundred percent certain that Becky Stein isn't *actually* reading my mind. I feel a bead of sweat roll down my neck.

"Bartok, yeah – the *Microcosmos* – 'Boating,'" I say.

"Why are you playing it in two instead of three?" Stein says.

There's a dry sober quality to his query. The question completely throws me off balance again. I rise to the occasion and offer him my response:

"Huh?"

"Look," he says. "This part is just the accompaniment – the part in three – the left hand before it switches to the right hand."

He sits at the piano.

"This theme here in the right hand is actually in two."

There's a generosity – a kindness in his voice that speaks to unlimited patience.

"See?" he says. And he plays.

And he counts while he's playing. And he's incredibly musical and I feel like a complete charlatan because I realize that I've become comfortable with my incorrect assessment of Bartok's intentions – I've become lazy – rather than *playing* the piano I've been playing *at* the piano. I've allowed the appearance of two sets of three eighth notes in the bass to lull me into a sleepy understanding of two sets of triplets instead of three sets of doublets, tempered, of course, with an awareness of the downbeat at the beginning of each measure, which encourages whatever buoyancy the music may have had through the perception of an unimpaired brain to dissipate and drag the whole thing to the bottom of Bartok's pond. I at once suspect my musical impairment – or my non-musical interpretation – has been the result of my almost continuous ingestion of meth and other drugs – a subject that I'm loath to address – especially now – simply because I've placed all my eggs for the time being, the time past and into the foreseeable future, into the dope basket. I've dug myself a rut musical, and social and every other –al– and furnished them all with dumpster furniture. My boat has sprung leak after leak until being dragged down into the muck.

Stein finishes the piece and turns to face me.

"May we see your product?" he asks.

I want to pull back on the reins for a minute, just to regroup, because I've been gut-punched by the unexpected. I want to further size up this Becky Stein and his friend – I'm still not sure what his name is – Kenyon – what kind of a name is Kenyon? And "Becky" too. Isn't that short for Rebecca? He doesn't seem like a queen – at least in my brief experience with him. The only thing I can think of that may have fostered this gender-confused name is something ethnic – maybe it's a Jewish thing, some orthodox nickname or something, like Bibi, and I quickly try to come up with a convincing syllogism about Jewishness and the last name Stein, but I don't know if my original premise is true, that all Steins are Jewish, which would make my conclusion that Becky Stein is therefore Jewish false – or at least unprovable given the dearth of knowledge I possess on the subject. As a matter of fact I don't *really* know if Stein is his last name.

All I've heard are stories about some dangerous guy named Becky Stein who's been known to shoot people to get his way. His last name could be McGillicutty for all I know. It seems that I know as much about onomatology as I know about Bartok. Plus I've never had the opportunity to socially entertain such an infamous gangster before either and I'm scrambling to come up with a plausible delaying tactic – *Would you like a nice cup of tea? Lemon or milk? Do I have any tea?* Nope. How about cookies? *Would you like a cookie?* There haven't been cookies in my house for months, if not years. What do I have? *Would you like a squirt of ketchup? It's just in the fridge – I think. I could garnish it with some that frozen shit on the walls of the freezer if you'd like. Maybe a bowl of Froot Loops with no milk? How about some real entertainment that doesn't have anything to do with playing the piano? Maybe the TV?* Probably not. I don't even have any porn, at least gay porn. I've allowed my elevated sensibilities to fuck me again. I hate gay porn. I'm completely bored with gay porn because it's so fucking *earnest* – probably because if it weren't earnest it would just be a bunch of queens fucking each other and that's not exactly sexy, so the porn actors are always growling at each other and being earnest cops or coaches or convicts who threaten to penetrate their victims with luggage-sized cocks, which we all know is what they wanted all along. I could offer to put on a tape of straight porn.

I have a couple of literal VCR videotapes of straight porn that I've been lugging around for decades – one that I purchased at the request of a young man I picked up on the street once who'd insisted on watching guys gangbang girls and shoot cum all over their faces, only after plowing them mercilessly for several minutes, content that I've since learned is requested by many so-called "straight" guys while they're having sex with other guys because, in the process of transference (mentally changing places with the porn characters on the screen), they imagine themselves to be the girls – no shit – a fact that's always been a mild disappointment to me, and is something that skirts the boundaries of victimhood: should I not also be entitled to occasionally have permission to perceive stereotypes performing their advertised roles? Regardless, I've been happy to accept the yoke of responsibility in these cases, and have even driven a young soldier fresh from the killing fields of Iraq, while both of us were screaming high on meth, to a twenty-four-hour Mexican swap meet where I paid for a slinky undergarment he called a "teddy," which he confessed to me mere minutes after meeting, that he wanted to wear while I fucked him silly. I have two other tapes: one I purchased because it had earned a place in the pantheon of campy weirdness, meaning that it featured several aging female porn actresses who'd seen better days, but they were making a comeback of sorts, and who, after spending a considerable amount of time lounging on seedy-looking couches in some motel room while wearing skimpy nighties, once their studly and much younger "dates" showed up, the most infamous of the actresses grabbed the horns of her impatience and spit out through clouds of cigarette smoke and with a substantial amount of gravel in her voice the phrase: "So you gonna fuck me or what!?" a demanding query that's always elicited a ton of guffaws from me and my friends. Then there's another tape that I may have that's just a study in the pathetic. It's this forty-something blonde-haired woman performing on stage for a smattering of degenerate men in some seedy theater purportedly located in San Francisco. Her performance consists of variations on what she could do with several ping-pong balls she'd stuffed up her vagina, all of which were designed to mimic some kind of vaginistic volcano that produces smoke (baby powder) and lava (hand lotion) and other surprisingly well-aimed ejaculates (who knows), a process that creates an amazing mess on the stage. The salient part of this tape wasn't the volcanic performance, but what she did after the show was over. Apparently (and pathetically) her contract included a codicil that required her, after all the erupting and whatnot, and after every last degenerate had exited the theater, while being cruelly illuminated by the raised house lights, to grab a container of 409 spray cleaner and a roll of paper towels and clean up the stage, which was now slick with bodily fluids and sexual detritus, all of which she did while still naked (except for a pair of stiletto high-heeled shoes), and which was recorded on the tape. What am I thinking? Even if I loved gay porn, or still owned a VCR machine, this is a dope deal. Stein wants to buy the shit and get the hell out of here.

I produce a sample and each man tastes it. There are a few nods.

"How much for two ounces," Stein says, to which I kind of

stammer, "$1,200." I'd originally wanted to charge $2,000, but Stein's personage has left me scrambling toward a hurried discount so that I can save face somehow.

We do the deal, and after a friendly handshake between us, all three men leave.

CHAPTER ELEVEN

The female section of the Cri-Life dining room, between the hours of 10:30 p.m. and 11:30 p.m. – at least five nights a week – is home to a ritual that the facility Administration members tacitly allow the mostly Hispanic gang-bangers who'd landed in Cri-Life directly from extended stays at various California prisons to hold: Spread, which is the monosyllabic equivalent of Sacred Banquet, suggesting not the verb "spread," but rather a noun that encompasses the panorama of sustenance and its attendant serving vessels that's "spread" over the surface of a tabletop and is available to all those who've been invited to partake, necessarily excluding any person of the female variety because of the ritual's provenance, which is the pretty much all male brand of penitentiary inmates, not to mention that pesky Non-Com rule that's pretty much omnipresent in the Cri-Life ether.

"Spread" actually consists of one of the long folding dining room tables that's been covered with paper plates and plastic spoons, all of which are symmetrically laid out to showcase the main event: a concoction of Ramen noodles and softened macaroni that's been mixed together while inside a large, black, heavy-duty plastic trash bag with hot tap water and generous amounts of ketchup and/or Tabasco sauce and/or salsa and/or about a quarter pound of salt and pepper and/or – depending on its availability, a whole jar of mayonnaise, and/or about a hundred thinly sliced canned hot peppers. This trash bag is somehow sealed shut and shaken by two or more said gang-bangers simply because it's too unwieldy for one guy to handle, then emptied into a large plastic mixing bowl. The trash bag is then discarded, apparently, because it's only plastic. There's an essential and charming bit of willful blindness that defines "Spread": Charity.

The spreaders – the guys putting on the banquet – have talked themselves into believing that this offering of food is somehow a charitable sacrifice of jealously hoarded foodstuffs to be distributed to those less fortunate, even though shortages of food at both state prison, the birthplace of the ritual, all the way to Cri-Life, where it's continued, are about as rare as paid-off BMWs tooling around the palm-lined avenues of Beverly Hills – even forgetting the most obvious fact that the food used in Spread is owned by the institution, which renders the only commodity capable of being provided charitably the good intentions of the spreaders, that and the time it's taken to prepare and showcase it. The intentional use of the plastic trash bag in which to mix the various ingredients of the feast locates Spread on the same level as faithful reenactment of any number of historical events, like people dressing up in Pilgrim suits to share early American Thanksgiving dinner with Indians, who shoot turkeys with bows and arrows and who eschew any newfangled European devices for food preparation in favor of what's traditionally been used by the natives. While they just as easily could have mixed the ingredients inside one of the available huge aluminum mixing bowls, a decision was made to use the plastic bag so as to retain Spread's authentic flavor. Flickering candles help to lend Spread its ritualistic air – not to mention a definite flavor of tender camaraderie, a detail that, to the uninitiated, seems to dangle its toes into the steamy waters of Lake Intimacy, which, along with its all male quality, imbues Spread with a pretty homoerotic flavor. On good nights, there's also several open loaves of both white and wheat bread, which is actually a nice touch, given the fact that what's in the bowl might not be sufficient quantities of carbohydrates to ingest just before beginning a night's sleep, or extrapolating back to the ritual's prison heritage, a night of crazy butt fucking, something that (it's hoped by the CDWs) would never happen inside the walls of Cri-Life.

Since his "honesty-tinged" performance at Step Study, Rogarth has moved past the anonymous label of "that new guy" to actually being recognized and acknowledged by name. He's bravely ventured out of his room and downstairs to the dining room for maybe a minute or two of TV news before bed, an infraction of the *Jesus/Recovery-Only-kind-of-media-to-be-exposed-to,-but-being-late-at night,-and-the-house-techs-being-by-now-completely-worn-down-because-*

they've-been-herding-residents-and-cataloguing-disputes-for-twelve-plus-hours-already,-they-allow-it-to-happen, and he's recognized by aforementioned gang-bangers, who, with an air of unmistakable solemnity and self-conscious generosity, invite him to partake of their bounty, with proffered paper plate brimming with red-tinted concoction along with a plastic spoon in outstretched hands: *Hey Holmes, join us for some Spread.* Almost automatically Rogarth accepts the plate of noodles, and right away realizes that this is a ritual of utmost seriousness and one that he's not dressed for. Rogarth is wearing worn Levis with holes at the knees and a misshapen stretched out t-shirt emblazoned with a Venn diagram on the front, the areas of colorful intersection designed to remind people seeing the shirt that the humble Mix Master, when used by members of certain populations, may serve as both ornament and instrument; while all the Mexicans are dressed in perfectly pressed chinos or Bermuda shorts and skin-tight white wife beaters with images of their wives and/or girlfriends and/or saviors and/or sons and daughters all interspersed with arcane numerals and/or letters/and/or signs signifying one's particular affiliation and number of deceased rivals, all peeking around their glistening biceps and/or neck and back muscles. Their shoes are pristine white Nikes worn over long tube socks that have been washed with a bleach-heavy mixture which suppresses even the tiniest divergence from the purest white that might soften their brightness. They're all recently showered and generously scented – they've literally dressed for dinner.

Rogarth, whose judgment has been temporarily knocked offline because of the veritable ocean of testosterone, tattoos and muscles and good will all seemingly aimed directly at him, realizes he's accepted the plate, even though he has yet to place both the plate and what's on it in any sort of accurate context. The idea occurs to him that rather than somehow being the object of an impossibly wonderful erotic dream, he's just expected to eat the food on the plate, much like that one time in Bordeaux when he mistook the traditional greeting from his handsome French tour leader, the one with the rough hands and two-days' growth, as an invitation to make out, so he opened his lips wide and stuck his tongue out mid-peck, an eyes-lightly-shut romantic swoon that Jean-Louie deflected with a practiced deftness, when he was really in the process of just saying hello.

Even though Rogarth has rallied, though, and after making the necessary adjustments to his perception, he decides not to demur, offering an unadorned "Thanks" before seating himself between Luis O., the forty-something tattooed banger with the generous rolls of cholesterol that bulge and hang over his belted shorts, and Tony B., that absolutely dreamy *I'd-do-him-in-a-fucking-heartbeat* stud, who often lingers towel-less outside the showers while standing in front of the bathroom mirror. And Rogarth slowly – distractedly – lifts a spoonful of noodles/macaroni to his mouth. *Tony B... I'm actually sitting next to Tony B.!,* his thoughts savoring the absolute chance of it all. Rogarth has never seen Tony smile – he's serious – "really" serious, though – not that kind of serious that some guys advertise while hulking around darkened gay bars, the guys with the huge muscles decorated with arcane-looking tattoos, tribal symbols that are supposed to contribute to some kind of a two-dimensional life of danger and/or hurt past, like white supremacist-whose-been-redeemed-because-after-beating-the-shit-out-a-defenseless-homo-he's-decided-to-go-ahead-and-taste-a-bit-of-the-cock-and-in-the-process-has-embarked-on-some-kind-of-redeeming-progressive-path-illumuminated-by-kind-of-spiritual-light instead of what they're really masking: an apron-clad housewife who's spent her afternoon primping and sipping cocktails a little – or a lot too early in the day – waiting for *that man o' mine* to either materialize for the first time or return home from his day selling pastel-colored shirts at Macy's.

Rogarth sighs while happily accepting the reality that Tony's persona is legitimate, and he finds that he has an overwhelming urge to help Tony out of his "darkness." Flawed? Injured? Rogarth imagines a subsequent moment of serendipity when maybe he and Tony B. will be alone – maybe out on weekend pass or something, even though Rogarth is aware of the House rules that dictate that passes must be made up of at least three residents – *three's a crowd, obviously* – but he allows his imagination to go there. Maybe the staff will acquiesce to allowing a duet to venture forth together – a harmless duet of "earnest" residents – after all, they've shown nothing but unvarnished eagerness to enjoy a life free from drugs and all they really want to do is to take a trip to the LA County Museum of Art – all the way down Highland on the bus and down Wilshire Boulevard. It's not like they planned for their third party to bow out – just the victims of circumstance. How could they – or anybody – have predicted Smith's stomach flu, which has confined him to his room, sweating and throwing up all day, which reduced the number of residents on the pass to two. And they actually did make an honest effort to recruit another member to accompany them on their outing – but to no avail. Recovery house residents are just as tribal as anybody in any population – and just as petty and mean, and weekend pass groups of three or four will sprout and grow prejudices against all others on an ad hoc basis. Just circumstances, really. They're good boys actually – why not make an exception – just this one time? They're responsible, aren't they? Yes, Rogarth thinks. We *are* responsible members of society, me and Tony. I won't be effusive on our private pass. I'll be a little aloof with him – can't seem too eager – too hungry. Don't want to spook him. We'll get a coffee at Coffee Bean – best to steer Tony into my sphere of influence with the little things at first. Guiding someone away from Starbucks is trickier than it seems sometimes, I mean, especially if they're used to Starbucks, like it's still some people's vision of moonlight. Hard to explain what my preference is based on. Okay. If Tony insists on Starbucks, then so be it: Starbucks it will be. But hopefully he won't object to my preference of trying Coffee Bean and Tea Leaf. Maybe one of their little sweet desserts with the coffee – one for each of us, of course – much too early for a *Lady and the Tramp* spaghetti slurping moment that ends in a happy little kiss. No – separate desserts and coffee – probably a caramel machiatto (my fave!) that will maybe awaken a childlike curiosity in Tony: "This is good, Holmes! I wish I'd known about this – what you call it? Caramel mach" – "Machiatto," I finish for him. He's looking at me adoringly with a broad honest smile: "I love it!" Then the museum, where I want to steer Tony right away to the Kandinsky stuff, even though it may seem horribly modern and unapproachable to him. But I'll still be there to guide him – to elicit intelligent questions from deep inside his naïve soul. "It's not representative, Tony. It's beautiful, no?

The shapes and their colors are just – there. Right? There's a kind of rhythm and tempo to them, I think. You know those words, right? Rhythm and tempo? Like in music? Arnold Schoenberg really admired Kandinsky and vice-versa. Oh, Schoenberg? A composer of twelve-tone music – from early twentieth century? Never mind!"

We're having a great time together – I catch Tony's expression of anxiety now and again as he steals glances at me – and I imagine a future time when we meet up on a forty-eight-hour pass – a practice that's strictly forbidden by Cri-Life, but what you gonna do when you're in love, right? And we get into bed together – just two really good friends (for now!) and I'm finding it hard to suppress my passion. My hand passes his crotch and there's no objection – no shrinking – just his sweet breath on my face. With practiced deliberation bordering on solemnity, I burrow under the bedclothes and make my way to his cock, which gets hard in a flash. And I'm sucking him – tenderly at first – me imagining what's going on in his mind. I continue for a few moments – he awkwardly fumbles to reach my hard cock too, and he's actually caressing my boner. It's heaven. I wedge my forearms between his thighs and push them apart slightly, then scoop his buttocks up, while, at the same time, I encourage the blankets to fall off our naked bodies. I add a bit of pressure onto his tightly closed asshole – and he squirms slightly when my forefinger crosses the threshold. His muscular legs close, forcing me out, something that I'm actually kind of relieved about. Plenty of time to explore there in the future. I'm actually glad he's said no – not like Elmer, that guy who was paroled to his mom's house across Avenue 43 after spending nine years in Corcoran.

It was much the same thing I'm currently having with Tony, but I was anything but sober at the time. I'd talked Elmer into slamming a good-sized shot of speed so that I could get "there" with him. I dove right for his cock, and after a minimum of protest, Elmer's legs opened wide, inviting me, trumpets blaring, as I made my entrance into his anal canal, which, it turned out, was a route about as untraveled as the 405 at rush hour. In about one second his ass opened to swallow my cock – and I'm sure would have had room to accommodate most of Van Nuys and Cincinnati as well. Either Elmer's the earth mother of ex-cons and just naturally has a sense of freedom about life and sex, which allows him to banish any and all objections about penetration in the service of pleasure – or he's spent the previous nine years taking enormous cocks into his ass, either or both of these possibilities having the ability to drain the blood from my cock and the intention from my heart. My remaining time inside Elmer's ass was kind of like flopping around inside a huge inflatable pool resting, all bloated and moldy, on a dying front lawn of brown grass in a shabby part of town. I withdrew my flaccid dick and headed forthwith to the shower to wash away the ickiness of the experience with him.

Rogarth really wants to comment on the food offered at Spread, but restrains himself, instead lifting spoonful after spoonful of noodles and macaroni into his mouth, knowing that a suggestion of maybe adding a side of *cornichons* to the meal might not be appreciated.

With unmistakable intention, Tony B. casually leans in to Rogarth's "space," and lays his arm over his shoulders, then whispers into his ear: "It's good, huh, Rogarth. You and me, Rogarth, right? To the hubs, huh?"

Rogarth's imagination again, right there in the dining room, takes flight, soaring up to the fluorescent lights on the ceiling, then darting to the deserted serving line with the Plexiglas guard, then performing virtuoso feats, slaloming between chair legs for the length of the room until he finds himself resting between Tony's legs staring at his still zippered fly. He finds himself between the horns of a dilemma, whether to respond demonstrably and give in to his desire, a decision that his imagination has already constructed the consequences for: either, right there on the spot, giving Tony B. the best blowjob of his life, something that would cause a Cri-Life upheaval similar to tectonic adjustment that would place Los Angeles smack dab into the Pacific, or practicing restraint. "Yeah," he says to Tony without turning his head.

"You gonna be my dog, Rogarth. You're my dog, right?"

There's a split second of indecision in Rogarth, which isn't lost on Tony, who's immediately constructed an exaggerated expression of profound disappointment on his face, a crestfallen look that Rogarth uses to construct a complete context that he can fit into. This is *kabuki,* Rogarth deduces. This is gangbanger *kabuki,* and he has a part to play.

"Yeah," he answers as he looks squarely into Tony B.'s eyes. "I'm your dog."

El Ocho is part of the Spread cohort, but he's remained silent for the duration of Tony's interaction with Rogarth. El Ocho smiles and nods, then helps himself to another plate of noodles.

CHAPTER TWELVE

The AIDS Clinic

It's Tuesday. Gallagher grips the wheel of the Cri-Life van. Sitting next to him is Shoshanna and behind her are Rogarth and Eric P. and behind them sits El Ocho, who, even though he's one of the few fiercely heterosexual guys of the gang-banger variety at Cri-Life with HIV, he wants to make it pretty clear to everybody, both inside the van and out, that he's not queer. His condition is closely guarded, so he never talks about it, either in Rick's Saturday morning support group, or in larger groups where men are encouraged to speak freely about why and how often they've beat and/or abandoned their wives and/or kids. One thing he truly dislikes is the interest his nickname – El Ocho – has fostered among most of the gay guys at Cri-Life, who spend a lot of time speculating on what exactly the "8" refers to. Shoshanna has HIV too, which she insists she caught from using dirty needles, a factoid that hardly has the ring of truth, given her considerable girth. The skin on her arms is pretty much pristine, which betrays the fact that even under the best of circumstances, and utilizing uncommon skill at finding viable veins, overweight people are almost impossible to hit. Not only are the veins obscured by layers of cellulite, they're tiny hair-like vessels that spider off, seemingly in an effort to resist scrutiny or puncture – so the Cri-Life AIDS cohort kind of doesn't buy her story – not that anybody really cares how she got it. Once you got it, you got it. It just seems silly to lie about it. She attends the HIV support group, and she dislikes Rick as much as anybody in the facility.

This is one of the few times when the House has agreed to let the AIDS residents drive themselves to the clinic, which has imbued this little errand with a holiday-like mien. Patients are usually driven there, dropped off and picked up after one of the more senior residents in the group calls for pick up. But Gallagher's Completion Date has been recorded, signed and blessed by just about everybody in North Hollywood, so he's been awarded the considerable responsibility of driving the van-full of residents himself.

As if he's behind the wheel of a sports car, Gallagher whips the behemoth van up into the medical center's driveway and has to slam on the brakes to keep from crashing through the lowered wooden arm that only raises to admit vehicles after the driver retrieves a proffered paper ticket from an automatic dispenser. There's a time stamp on the ticket, and on the reverse side is the parking company's name and logo – *Secure Park* or *Secure-Easy-Park (which should actually read Profit Park)* along with *Thank You* at the bottom. El Ocho approves of Gallagher's driving, as evidenced by some vague utterance of endorsement to somebody named Holmes. Shoshanna yells "motherfucker" and Rogarth just braces himself against the armrest. Eric wants to scream, but he resists the urge and just giggles nervously.

The whole group de-vans, walks through the darkened parking structure and out across the sunny area where the doctors and clinic staff park their deluxe cars, and through the building's front door, which is overtly unassuming, and into the jumbo-sized Otis manufactured elevator, the kind that most buildings of fewer than five floors use.

It's the kind of elevator that seems to have been designed as an implement to finally choke any remaining joy from that process often thoughtlessly labeled as life, and fosters effects not unlike hopeful, wide-eyed children learning that both Santa Clause and the Easter Bunny have been rendered dead and stinking fictitious constructs of parental imagination. This only becomes apparent *after* everybody is inside the elevator and the button for the desired floor has been pushed. It's a regressive experience. Instead of being quickly, efficiently and sometimes thrillingly whisked skyward, as is the experience in elevators in most skyscrapers, time is intentionally retarded inside an Otis. The doors meander their way to the "shut" position, which, in itself, isn't all that objectionable when viewed as a prelude to a hoped for speedy ride of efficiency. But even after the doors have closed, there's a couple of moments of elevatorial rumination: after having arrived at the locked position, it's as if the mechanism is recapping every single necessary step in its safety-first checklist before signaling to the motor's cable mechanism to begin to rise or descend, a signal that's reluctantly received and acknowledged with a mechanical groan and more than a little un-confidence building shuddering. The elevator begins to ascend, but not happily, the message being: *if I must.* The frustration quotient of Otis elevator rides is only compounded if one's destination is floor four or five, and other patients or customers or clients or whatever have pushed buttons two or three, in which case you begin to judge their characters as those of the impossibly lazy variety because if it were you, you'd just as well have taken the stairs.

Finally, Gallagher's group exits the elevator and heads to the clinic's inconspicuous entrance door, with just a number as signifier; nothing that says Such-and-Such AIDS Clinic Enter Here, and one can begin to sense the influence of federal HIPPA (Health Insurance Portability and Accountability Act) regulations designed to maintain an impregnable wall of privacy designed to thwart any prying eyes, which gives the place a secret police kind of flavor.

The chilliness of the room makes all who enter wish they'd worn fur-lined parkas. Two handsome youths, minority flavored, radiating purpose, tinged with humility, look directly at you from a large flat screen television affixed to the wall. They're both wearing vague smiles, and their teeth, which are firmly planted in beds of healthy pink gums, are enviably straight and white; their clothes are clean. The boys exude an energy suggestive of nothing except an easy relationship with each other, with their audience and with the world; they project the sense that they're touched with the courage necessary to propel them through impending adversity, or that they've just escaped certain doom relatively unscathed – "relatively" because let's be frank: AIDS isn't exactly a butt-load of lilacs and sequins. The boys seem to be hovering around a shiny old car – or maybe a waffle iron; perhaps a book of some sort – it's not even clear if they're inside their living room or out in the wilderness. It doesn't matter though because the gist of this video scene is that they've met the scourge of disease by drawing from the fount of good will and pragmatism that's available to everyone who visits this clinic. And they're flourishing – they're brave. The implicit message seems to be: *You too can experience life as we do, if you do as we've done.*

As they continue with their easy grins and focus-starved gazes while still hovering around each other, a robust woman's voice, wise, compassionate, slightly smoky, provides context. She is speaking Spanish, and one suspects she's saying something about the clinic like: "At [insert name of clinic here] our knowledgeable and professional staff of board-certified doctors, competent nurses, assistants, social workers and office staff are here to provide the very best of care to HIV-impacted people living in Los Angeles, regardless of their ability to pay." This is probably what she's saying because of the widely recognized Spanish expression for AIDS – *el Sida* – peppers her speech, but mostly because this is the *Español* side of this particular loop that alternates with the English version of the video, which most of the flip-flop wearing obese transvestites, pious AA acolytes, gin-sipping dowager empresses, black do-rag wearing hip-hop thugs, skinny love-struck cha-cha queens with the most elaborate ring tones, and toothless, gum-gnashing S&M tweakers with puffed up protease inhibitor veins on their legs, all stuffed into the waiting room, have seen it about a thousand and one times.

One by one the Cri-Life cohort is called in to be weighed and have his or her blood pressure and temperature measured and recorded, then sent back out to wait to be assigned to an Examination Room. Both Rogarth and Gallagher know better than to give in to their impatience and lodge a complaint with the office staff about the nearly ninety minutes they've been waiting to be called in to see a doctor – there's more than one usually. Rogarth shifts his weight in his chair and continues watching the AIDS video.

The only reading materials are printed versions of the video, but they're mostly all in Spanish, so all Rogarth or Gallagher or Shoshanna can do is identify some common Spanish words that everybody knows: 'ahora' = now; 'para' = for; 'quando' = how much – probably – which is kind of like finding yourself in a scary part of town and anemically waving to the smattering of people whom you recognize because you shop at the same market, hoping they'll recognize you too. And, of course, you can always admire the photographs of sizzling hot boys who the publishers of this tract want its readers to believe have AIDS, but they're probably models who have a standing-room-only crowd of T-cells stampeding through their veins.

One/third of the complete body of a full-figured nurse appears in the doorway that leads to the examination rooms, and without looking up she calls out Rogarth's name, who tosses the magazine he's reading, one of the few in English, the one called *Poz,* with its surprisingly candid articles that describe sexual practices without any use of irony or metaphor at all, onto the little side table. The language in *Poz* is as straightforward as it gets, explaining, under the harsh illumination of the editorially borne necessity of pragmatism, the properties utilized by quantifiable thrusts and their attendant amounts of friction created by the average-sized penis against the walls of the average-sized rectum in both the standing position and prone – along with assumptions and admonishments regarding the overall health of the anal canal, which again is spelled out in unvarnished descriptions either of anal walls that are blemish-free or which are scarred with either hemorrhoids or anal warts and/or their attendant damaged tissue – descriptions that explain just how easy or difficult HIV-tainted sperm will find it to finally infect a targeted CD-4 cell. These magazines always contain five-to-seven page offerings invariably titled "Blowjobs: Safe or Not?" which Rogarth – and probably at least ninety percent of homos who're reading the magazine – pass up because they've drawn the line somewhere. Rogarth will yield to injunctions from practicing unsheathed anal sex, but absolutely refuses to give up sucking dick, and won't even consider for a moment – even if it's been deemed "preferable" by the expert class – sliding a latex-clad penis into his mouth, something he's acquiesced to a couple of times when dealing with overly paranoid-because-they-fancy-themselves-members-of-some-kind-of-unsullied-social-stratum-like-cops-or-heterosexual-married-guys, and is an experience that he equates with sucking on a dildo.

Rogarth hates to dredge up certain memories, but he'd allowed himself, years earlier, to be coerced, while elbow deep in various leather-tinged sexual get-togethers, into sucking on a dildo that was offered to him by some G-string clad, muscle-bound fake cop, and who placed all his sexual/social capital into some vague category he referred to as *nasty*. Rogarth does, however, take some degree of solace in imagining himself to be just a minor member of a much larger group of the general population who've sucked on a fake cock. He's pretty sure that Warren Buffet or even Hillary Clinton, during rare or even not-so-rare moments of exceedingly private sexual abandon, has slurped on the occasionally proffered latex molded *ersatz* penis.

He stands and follows the nurse through the doorway. "Room number three," she says, and watches as Rogarth heads inside the third examination room where, instead of hopping up onto the examination table, he seats himself in the chair opposite the doctor's computer workspace and chair, which, for now are still vacant. Rogarth has made this decision so that he can stand and offer his hand to the doctor when he/she enters, something that he considers more dignified than having to either sit, with legs dangling over the side of the examination table, with extended hand, or to jump down, shake hands, then reseat himself onto the tabletop: *Hi, nice to see you.* In Rogarth's mind, sitting in this chair flattens the doctor/patient paradigm into a more co-equal status, because he's just about had enough of the godlike perch doctors occupy in the United States social hierarchy. He's also pretty sure, though, that even this tiny gesture of protest will be recognized by the doctor as a condition described over several pages of medical school text books in chapters titled "Dangers and Trends Exhibited by Problem Patients and Their Underlying Meanings," which, he fears, would co-locate his presenting problems in both the medical literature that deals with HIV, and also that enormous tome of mental problems called the *DSM-V or VI*, depending on how many Porsches or Lamborghinis freshly minted Southern California psychologists or psychiatrists have purchased on 500-month contracts. The thought of being referred to a psychiatrist makes Rogarth's eyes glaze over and he yawns, and he actually considers whether or not it would be advisable to climb up on the table, stretch out and take a little snooze while waiting for the physician. Fuck it, Rogarth thinks, as he settles further into the chair. It's too cold to sleep anyway, and he briefly imagines legions of blood thirsty bacteria making a continuous assault on this clinic, an assault that remains a futile exercise because of the impenetrable wall of chilliness fending them off.

To kill time, he studies the graphic posters interspersed on the wall that are nearly all overly colorful representations of both the human immunodeficiency virus itself and the treatments available to suppress its advancement. A couple of the posters with pictures of the virus could be, Rogarth opines to himself, a cross between the work of Paul Klee and Wassily Kandinsky, except with textual explanations of the shapes and the processes they're involved in: *Fusion of HIV to the host cell surface, Host Cell, HIV RNA, reverse transcriptase, integrase and other viral proteins enter the host cell, Viral DNA is formed by reverse transcription, Viral DNA is transported across the nucleus and integrates into the host DNA*...and so on.

It's safe to say that Rogarth – and probably most other patients who study these posters – have never really imagined these processes taking place inside their own bodies, probably because envisioning such stuff seems like a pointless and self-defeating exercise, unless, of course, in the process of contextualizing HIV/AIDS in particular and Disease in general, one relies on the dubious wisdom of people like Deepak Chopra, who, in his self-conscious good health and wealthy/creative social standing, can (and often does), ex cathedra, dispense opinions that lay responsibility of actually being afflicted by HIV on some kind of metaphysical/spiritual deficiency rather than as simply the result of a biological process, which, in the United States of America, truthfully speaking, suggests a healthy dose of injecting drugs into veins by way of dirty needles or, god forbid, unprotected butt-fucking, something that betrays the fact that Ms. Chopra doesn't party that often and probably doesn't care for fags all that much either.

Just above and off to the side of the blood pressure machine is a gigantic poster haphazardly and pretty thoughtlessly conceived and executed that contains mostly textual elements – lists to be exact – along with enough graphic components to make it seem crowded – explanatory pictures of happy, healthy people who've maintained an unwavering routine of prescribed pill-taking, along with the instruments that help them to remember their regimens: calendars and pill containers sectioned off in both days of the week and hours of the day. Overlaying the pictures of the pill containers are brightly colored cloud-shaped textual notices that exhort people to "Ask your nurse! Ask your Nutritionist! Available FREE at the nursing station!" Doctors, it's not difficult to imagine, during brainstorming sessions where final decisions were made about the content of this poster, more than likely put the ix-nay on any text that included the suggestion to "Ask your Doctor!" because doctors would simply tell their patients to ask their nurses, etc. The creators of this poster wisely chose not to include any graphic examples of people who'd forgotten to take their meds for any number of reasons, the main one being that protease inhibitors haven't been around *that* long, and memories of the legions of walking dead are still fresh enough that people don't need to be reminded of them. Interspersed throughout the examination room – and the clinic as a whole – are cute wicker baskets ornamented with paper cutouts of daisies and smiling suns with radiating sunbeams, and which are overflowing with free-for-the-taking condoms packaged in a kind of pathetic clutching-to-nihilism genre of decoration featuring heavy metal lightning bolts emanating from oversized, glowering, corroded conduits suggesting that they're the vehicles best able to bear the dark sludge of some scary form of doom – along with explanations and warnings spelled out in misshapen fonts, all of which is designed, one can only imagine, to minimize any residual "dork" quotient that's earned by unfurling a rubber sheath down over the length of your cock before taking the anal plunge.

Since his time at Cri-Life, and awash in his newly minted identity of "good citizen," Rogarth, as he regards with a certain level of disdain the banks of unopened drawers lining the doctorless examination room, repeats to himself the phrase publicly uttered to the ranks of rarified journalists of musical periodicals by one Raisa Levine, the hermit-like dowager of Julliard and exponent of Schubert's piano music, who'd condescended a visit to the Golden State before she quickly turned tail and made a bee line back to New York City, her beloved metropolis whose storied support for Art with a capital 'A' was, even during Mme. Levine's golden years, being wrested from the purview of artists like herself and into the clutches of that vulgar class of promoters known as the Impressarios of Broadway – a trend that continued past Levine's death when impressarios began to be replaced by hedge fund managers whose artistic acumen made possible the seemingly endless panorama of marquis trumpeting the works of Walt Disney instead of Ibsen – a shit sandwich, one can only imagine, that would have provided the same degree of resonance to Mme. Levine as the atonal albeit outdated music of Xanakis as its elements, while attempting to be appreciated, bounced off her Romantically-inclined ear drums, and which Mme. Levine banished to the same realm of annoyance as that of any obstinate mosquito who was determined to ruin her Central Park picnic, so fuck you, California, you unnatural desert wasteland with your pathetic allegiance to green energy, pretension to art...and *money*, with thick Russian accent: *"There is nothing for me here."*

Rogarth is content, sober, agenda-less and alone and unwatched with just himself and his seemingly endless patience, to wait amid banks of unlocked medical drawers brimming with unwanted syringes and imagined injectables.

Immediately following a tiny knock, the examination door opens and in walks Dr. J. Dawa, who smiles and inquires: "Hi – how are you?" before seating himself opposite Rogarth's chair. Dr. Dawa's one of the few overtly gay doctors at this clinic, which has caused Rogarth – and more than a few of the stricken homos here – to wonder about the composition of the medical team staffing what's understood to be a clinic with an unusually high number of homos as its clientele. Either, Rogarth thinks, many of these doctors are hiding their gayness really well, or their curiosity about the study and treatment of HIV outweighs their dislike of gay guys, or they actually like gay guys so the HIV component is just a happy coincidence, or they're truly altruistic and they like everybody and they just want everybody everywhere to be healthy. But Dr. Dawa's certainly gay – he's known in the community as "Giggles" because he's always laughing at his own jokes – not really jokes, but what are really just run-of-the-mill observations about life in the USA that he seems to think are amusing enough to share a laugh about as they occur – but being just plain old observations, there are tons of them, so he's pretty much giggling all the time. Rogarth has a certain empathy for Dr. Dawa, though, not so much because of his giggling, but because of the way Dr. Dawa walks. Gay guys are often ID'd as gay because of how they carry themselves, a walking style that is at once gravity-defying and incredibly preoccupied. The "gay" walk often begins and ends with acknowledgement of its breeziness, but not for Dr. Dawa, whose style of walking Rogarth has speculated, is similar, if not identical, to the kind of walk Rogarth himself spawned one unfortunate night of blazing LSD tripping down at the beach at Point Mugu at a time when he was on the verge of dropping out of high school and a time when he had yet to "come out" as a gay individual. At the height of this acid trip, while surrounded by a motley group of other high-school dropouts composed of both males and females, all of whom were fiercely heterosexual (or such was Rogarth's belief), the entire group decided to brave a stroll down to the nearby jetty, a trip that necessitated traversing a section of beach that was covered with stones whose geologically sharp and adolescent angles had been worn smooth due to millennia of waves breaking over them – and were themselves merely a reflection of a ubiquitous process, not only in terms of expanse of time, but also the very nature of matter itself: stars – planets – moons – asteroids – mountains – cliffs – boulders – rocks – stones – pebbles – smaller pebbles – sand, a process not unlike AIDS survivors who've spent varying lengths of time imagining their own diminished selves, and waiting and waiting, fearing that their *bodies – minds – perception – consciousness* will, bit by bit, fall away, and who always seem to escape awareness of themselves – because life goes on or what the fuck ever – because you gotta wash the dog or wash some dishes – or take your pills – anyway, stuff seems to force its way into anybody's diminished view of the world unless you just fucking don't give a shit – about anything. And just like human beings, this process of geographic erosion has rendered these smooth, glistening, convex shapes of plump ovals and circles resting on beds of their own smaller and distant future selves as completely invisible to anyone whose various preoccupations have allowed them to be perceived as anything beyond just stones on the beach – or people on a bus – or anything capable of accepting, with a minimum of protest, the label "generic." And this is the salient part of potent LSD and the concealment – or willful overlooking – of one's gay tendencies: the truth about who you really are will come out, manifesting itself in what's directly in front of you. Just like Republicans, whose belief systems are so strongly entrenched and shabbily supported, the moment their eyes open in the morning, that doubt about life or existence or anything simply dissolves, making way for one overriding, life-affirming thought when their eyes alight on anything, be it a window sill, a toilet bowl or a cartoon program on television: *I thought so,* LSD will commandeer the most obvious element within the nascent homosexual's considerably impaired LSD-shaped field of vision in order to have its way about one's "essence." About two feet into the section of beach covered with these smooth stones, Rogarth, whose homosexual experiences, up to that point in his life were pretty much all in his head, began to imagine that the faces of this multitude of thousands of glistening, rounded stones peeking through the surface of the wet sandy beach were actually the very tips of the heads of giant erect penises – thousands and thousands of big beautiful cocks just waiting to be caressed and kissed and licked and sucked and – *Jesus fucking Christ it's getting hot out here* – which were somehow buried deep down in the sand, something that if actually the case would have clipped even the lumbering testosterone-fueled swagger of John Wayne into an overly careful mincing try-to-remain-aloft-for-as-long-as-possible-with-each-step gait because – well, it's obvious: stepping on the head of anybody's dick would hurt like hell. That, and the abject reverence that had begun to fuel, at that exact moment, Rogarth's curiosity about just what cock must really taste like, coupled with the thought of exactly how many cocks – beyond his own – actually exist on planet earth, a thought that became the catalyst for Rogarth considering, the first time in his life, the nature of infinity. It's taken near constant vigilance for the better part of a decade, but Rogarth has, for the most part, been able to "cure" himself of this walk, but it hasn't often been easy, especially when he forgets himself due to being higher than fuck. His unimpaired time at Cri-Life has helped him to keep the loftiness of his walk at bay, which allows him to silently judge Dr. Dawa's walk unreservedly.

Rogarth has deduced that AIDS doctors are required to ask certain questions, one of which is the old standby: "Any thoughts of suicide since we talked last?" which Dawa faithfully utters.

Dawa is poised at his computer keyboard to enter Rogarth's response into the more than likely medical database administered from both Sacramento and Washington D.C. – or wherever the CDC's offices are, like Georgia or Alabama – that his computer terminal is currently connected to.

Rogarth wants to foreshorten this part of the examination, but for some reason he decides to tell the truth: "*Of course I have.*" He wants to add *you fucking moron,* but decides that that prolongation would simply serve as the catalyst for unspeakable and unknowable layers of complication that, for some weird, reason-defying subroutine that's worthy of study in some humanities class focusing on *genre,* would manifest itself in the inevitable yet regrettable weaponization of etiquette where recitations of discontent become manifested as please-and-thank-you-laden observations that serve to funnel the complainant's morsels of displeasure, like cattle herded to their deaths while dutifully tramping up and down various ramps leading to a killing room, into a no-win realm of argument and to its ultimate proclamation: *there is no way I can answer that question, sir* – and which will usually not only raise your blood pressure to the aneurism level, but also launch yourself right into a locked 5150 box somewhere in a downtown jail, and has the same effect as calling time out so that you can don a pair of fluffy, feather-filled fake boxing gloves before punching the beatific grin right off some idiot's face.

Nevertheless, Rogarth's candidness forces Dawa to ask follow-ups, beginning with a slightly anxiety-tinged: "Please explain."

Rogarth wants to shake Dawa by his shoulders because he's been saddled with the responsibility of explaining the unexplainable. He wants to display his arms scarred from shooting dope:

How the fuck should I know, you idiot! I shoot dope into my arms. I can't speak for everybody – because I don't know everybody, but I'm thinking that we, meaning dope fiends, on some level, all want to die, but we're so fucking scared of just about everything that we don't want to make a mistake as we traverse that yawn-inducing tapestry that's too often generously described as life, which is why overdoses are such an attractive alternative to maybe blowing your brains out with a shotgun in the mouth, like we're all little

Hitlers who try to escape the responsibility of actually committing a reprehensible act by labeling it the product of offering to ourselves and then accepting a fait accompli, whether it's the annexation of the Sudatenland or the injection of too much dope into a vein: Oops! Too late now, I guess. Pity – I would have made a helluva forty-year-old. As if – really as if, motherfucker – one could or would have the wherewithal to assign a value to the sudden realization that an overdose was either a) happening, or b) finishing – which probably would depend on what kind of dope you're using – heroin taking on the role of guillotine with all its sudden finality, and even if you could squeeze out an opinion while sinking into that particular blackness, one would be hard pressed to give a fuck because perceived dying just doesn't matter that much because you're feeling so warm and fuzzy and pretty fucking sleepy – or cocaine, which affords a pretty sharp and accurate awareness of your organs going all numb inside your body, one by one, and the surprising onset of paralysis, which doesn't allow you to even scream for your boyfriend (lucky you!) 'Hey…I need help here. I think I'm dying,' or, if you think you're keeping your drug use a secret, propriety would dictate that, dying or not, you should keep your mouth shut, a circumstance that lends a slight tinge of noble (at least temporarily) purpose to your paralytic silence. Some dope fiends would add overdoses of methamphetamine here, but I'm not convinced that bona fide overdoses can be caused by using too much of the shit, which, rather than causing death, too much meth makes your eyeballs bulge and shake like crazy. Or it just may be that suicide is the natural response to the unshakable and inescapable frustration that comes from the realization that dreams are what it's all about. "Yes, that's right, Rogarth! Good boy! To be or not to be, or more plainly, to dream or not to dream! Please continue." Because if dreams are what we're here for, then it stands to reason – please fucking stop me if you have the answer – that the more dreaming the better? Isn't that it? And please don't hit me with 'it's a matter of degree.' Please! I couldn't handle that bullshit one more fucking time.

###

Knowing that this observation is probably insufficient as an explanation of a planned suicide, Rogarth instinctively tries to mentally prepare to resolve the looming *chicken-or-the-egg; cause-and-effect* dilemma. As if his mind were a Rolodex, Rogarth considers and reviews the multitude of "salient" memories of inciting incidents throughout his life, being careful to gloss over the Epidemic because he's decided it's just too fucking obvious, and for some reason his brain alights on his earliest, meaning teenaged, recognition of profound joy brought on by serendipitous events, which time has eroded into – due to shifting appetites and prejudices – just another memory that he'd prefer had never happened.

Rogarth doesn't really have a clue whether this is relevant to the suicide question, but for the moment he feels obliged to remember a certain afternoon when he was listening to a Bach cantata, the Easter or the Christmas – or maybe even *St. Matthew's Passion* – while sitting on the edge of his single bed nestled inside his parents' suburban ranch-style house with all that quilted, color-coded artwork, used brick, and avocado green carpet – and, through the window of his bedroom, he looked up to the sky, which was enjoying a period of breathless calm between hostile bouts of a violent springtime storm. At exactly the place in the music where an oboe solo took flight and began to glide majestically – (can something be lonely and majestic at the same time?) – over a comforting bed of appropriate harmonies that shimmered and shifted according to some terrible cosmic pattern, a swarm – it might be better to say "flock" because "swarm" drips with the foreboding portent of misfortune because locusts and boils and hail and shit, and "flock" is more like saying "bouquet" rather than "bunch" – but it was a swarm – a straight up swarm of birds – probably starlings, whose miraculous flight, seemingly afforded by the safety of surprisingly generous patches of blue sky interspersed between outcroppings of glowering gray storm clouds – in joyous concert with Bach's intentions, exactly – *exactly* mirrored the shape of the music, swooning and soaring and shifting shapes that tyrannically followed the music's strict metronomic meter, an experience that was curious, awe inspiring and intimate all at the same time and was so profound that Rogarth at once banished it to a protected place deep inside. But the memory itself was quickly overshadowed by the reality of his human condition. Even sensing the importance of this musical moment that had allowed him to fleetingly glimpse a cosmic benevolence that he was certain could resolve all manner of human-born earthly problems, he, out of abject laziness, never bothered to relocate the music so that he might reproduce this phenomenon again, something that's always invoked a sense of shame in him.

Short of sharing this memory with Dr. Dawa, though, this is what Rogarth said:

"Nah, Doc – I'm just bullshitting you about the suicide. I wanna live."

"You're sure?"

"Yeah."

"That's a relief."

"So what's the prognosis, doc?"

"No one really knows, but we hope – don't we – for a full life."

"Where I can be healthy and get a job a buy a house and a car and all that?"

"Well, yeah."

"And live to be – what? Sixty?"

"Oh, don't stop there!"

"Seventy? Eighty?"

"Pretty lucky, huh…"(breathy giggling). "You using protection during sex?"

"Huh?"

"Sex. I changed the subject. You practicing safe sex?"

Rogarth imitates Dawa's breathy giggle. Dawa cocks his head.

"Sorry," Rogarth says. "I'm not having sex. I'm in a treatment facility."

"Oh, yes," Dawa says while scrolling down through his computer notes on Rogarth. "What's it called again? Cry…?"

"It's with an 'I'…a made-up acronym. Chrysalis something or other – Chrysalis Rendevouz Inhabitant or some bullshit."

Dawa giggles. "Sounds awful. So no screwing at this place?"

"Nope."

"Must be hard. There's no real evidence that you won't be able to grow old like your parents or your grandparents, Rogarth."

"Sounds great."

Dawa considers offering Rogarth a morsel of counseling, but his time is valuable. He's abruptly all business, telling Rogarth he's going to issue instructions for the nursing staff to give him vaccinations against pneumonia, meningitis and also a flu shot before Rogarth must head back to Cri-Life, and offers a frilly wave of his hand before ducking out of the examination room.

CHAPTER THIRTEEN

Jimmy S. emerges from the restroom at the Arco station up on Sunset Boulevard, the one right next to that failed strip mall at La Brea. He's washed his face and actually run his thick red hair under the faucet in the bathroom's sink – it's obvious that he's been trying to refresh himself and appear less like a walking corpse than he appeared a few minutes previous. He still looks like shit, but at least he feels a little better – and god knows he's had enough sleep to sustain him for a while. He feels a certain regret at having refused Korn's invitation to get some burritos at Antonio's because he knows he should eat something. But he's on his way to see The Geisha over on Martel, and he's hopeful that she'll be awake, that she'll remember to buzz him up – and most of all that he'll be able to squeeze a shot of speed out of her – one last time – at least that's been his strategy for the last half dozen or so times he's been to see the little queen. Jimmy's forgotten The Geisha's real name – it wasn't anything Asian – something like Brian or Brendon or something like that, but because he spends almost all his time dressed in kimonos and other slinky Oriental-looking robes, Jimmy and a bunch of other guys have just learned to refer to him as The Geisha.

Jimmy tries to fortify himself as he approaches Sunset Boulevard. In order to reach the other side of this major thoroughfare he's going to have to cross it, a task whose unpleasantness quotient, especially the older he gets, has grown to fearful dimensions simply because Jimmy fancies himself a mind reader, especially when it comes to the drivers and passengers of cars stopped not only at that particular red light, but all the red lights of the city. He just absolutely knows he's going to be judged (it really doesn't matter if he's being judged fairly or unfairly in this case – he just wishes they'd stop looking at him.) Jimmy reluctantly presses the button on the light standard and hopes he'll be joined by others before the crossing begins so that the attention searing into him will hopefully be dispersed between him and any other human beings on this asphalt journey between lines of the crosswalk. But he's alone. His only other option is to appear as generic as possible, a strategy he's practiced hundreds of times over the years, and is one that all other non-human creatures on earth have perfected because it allows them to wake up to yet another glorious breakfast of worms or plankton or krill or – actually anything but Twinkies, apparently because the "lower" animals instinctively sense that what won't nourish them will probably harm them – or worse, bore them to inattentiveness. But whether it's a matter of burned out memory neurons or a Darwinian survival mechanism, Jimmy doesn't remember that this "disappearing" technique he's gearing up for at the moment usually has exactly the opposite effect than what he'd planned: Halfway across such a huge intersection Jimmy tries to will everything about himself to flatten into plainness: his facial features, the length and depth of his gait, the height and weight of his steps, the fit of his pants and shirt, the way the folds of his clothes behave, the object of his gaze, his gel-infused well-wrought hairstyle, his *intentions* – gravity itself – everything that he can think of, the sum of which is Jimmy S. – all of it devolves into the exact inversion of his hugely successful performance of imitation that results in him becoming aware that the only judgment that can possibly be made by others looking at him is: *Oh, look at that guy! He's pretending to be human!*, a realization that, once it's acknowledged, compounds exponentially, and has in the past resulted in Jimmy, with bulging eyes and the fierce albeit short-lived resentment often embodied by the underdogs of society – at least the ones who at one time had a choice in the matter, directing his gaze back at all the haters in their cars: *You satisfied now, motherfucker!?* Either that or its inverse where, like a forlorn puppy who's close to tears, he beseeches that girl in the Chevy Malibu or that businessman in the VW, or that bus full of students – all those drivers – to please – *please stop it; that he only wants to cross the street.* In such instances, though, he knows better than to ask the looming question: *Why? Why are you looking at me?* because he's conflicted. He is at the same time both really quite afraid and also quite thoroughly hopeful of being shown mercy by some vehicle-bound good Samaritan who might want to hear about his problems, because he doesn't think he could resist the temptation of making an act of confession to a perfect stranger – right there in the middle of Sunset Boulevard:

###

I'm flawed. I know I fucked up over at Point Mugu a couple of decades back. I couldn't help it – I was just driving up the PCH – I know I should think things through more of the time – I know I shouldn't have taken my clothes off in front of the giant sand dune where we used to get drunk. But I thought I had to, I really did, like my salvation depended on it. But – my imperfections are almost certainly more deep-seated than stripping out on the PCH at one in the morning, even though it *was* pretty fucking cold that night, so maybe that's it, but maybe not. Oh – okay, I got it now. It's my nails. I knew that was gonna come up sooner or later. I should have stopped picking at them decades ago. As a matter of fact, I'm absolutely the only person I know – at least of dope fiends whom I care to hang out with – who still does that. I rarely chew them – never got into that because chewing suggests more of a commitment than peeling does because when you pick and peel them, you can hide with your hands in your lap or wherever, but chewing them – that's really not giving a damn. Your shit's right out there for everybody to see. Maybe it's that little seemingly insignificant detail, the one that's allowed me to hide my imperfections in my lap where I've spent – I haven't added up the time, but it's probably, all together, maybe about between six months and ten years that I've picked and peeled my way to freakdom. And it's not like I don't notice other peoples' nails when they're all fucked up either. I do. And I judge, but it's the kind of judging done by the guilty, because my nails are almost always more screwed up than theirs. And I suspect this habit is going to turn out to be something listed on my death certificate: "Decedent's nails chewed" but there won't be any way I can explain, after I'm dead, that chewing with my teeth wasn't my vehicle of choice in the process of willful disfigurement of this part of my body. The dead can explain exactly zero, except on TV, and that's a whole other story that's made some asshole hundreds of millions of dollars and sold millions of Fords and tons of hand sanitizer and created shiny new CSI curricula at expensive storefront schools that promise rewarding careers of employment after only a short eight months of earnest study. And people *will* judge me. If I'm murdered, probably the first thing the coroner will notice – beyond my prodigious number of track marks – is my raggedy nails: "He's a nail picker, detective...one of the more egregious cases I've seen actually." Or what's more likely, death due to an overdose, where chewed up nails is just one in the pantheon of expected bad habits that the hopelessly immature citizen is expected to suffer. It might even be mentioned at my memorial service: "If only Jimmy'd stopped picking his nails to death. Maybe he'd still be here with us." Picking a tiny chink loose on one of my nails, then peeling it off just gives me so much pleasure. How to explain the urge to continue doing this past the fourth grade...hmmm. It's really kind of an invitation to attend to something – what's it called? An exigency. What a fucking great word. Really, an invitation to attend to an exigency. And if you're anything like me, real invitations, like to attend parties or weddings or whatever, more robust invitations that involve good-natured interaction with other, you know, human beings, started drying up a long time ago. It's kind of like when you have a loose tooth in front – either upper or lower – and the tooth is still pretty firmly there, but still it's a little bit loose. It's that fucking tongue, that muscle of deft curiosity that leaps to action as soon as it's discerned even a slight imperfection inside the mouth – and a loose tooth, to this instrument of Babel, amounts to an insatiable curiosity where testing the tooth's viability about one billion times per day isn't unreasonable. Not only isn't it unreasonable, it actually seems like it's a duty. If it weren't for speech, it would probably be reasonable to say that the tongue is the body's tool for detecting and verifying imperfections inside the mouth – and testing and verifying over and over and over until a loose tooth can't take it anymore and just falls out. I'm not an idiot. I know that nail picking can never rise to the level of vocation, avocation – or even hobby. How fucking dumb would that be – "Oh, my hobby? Yeah, I have a 'hobby.' It's picking my nails down to the quick." Like if I was ever on a TV game show for gay guys where some single guy chooses a date from just the aural/oral evidence that three contestants would offer, meaning that the choice couldn't be based on anything visual anyway. "Oh, I'll take bachelor number three because he picks his nails." So that's what my little habit of picking at my nails is like. So I'm sorry. I'm really fucking sorry I never got around to putting Band-Aids around the imperfection on my left thumb's nail just to allow it to grow to its potential. Either that or maybe opting instead for a more punishment-heavy medieval routine where forbidden bad habits are stopped by turning their pleasure quotient into awfulness, like maybe soaking the tips of my fingers in vinegar overnight – or here's a good one: maybe jamming my thumb up my ass several times a day. But that still leaves the other less opposable digits to bask in their – maybe not fragrant, but unspoiled states. I suppose I could learn to fist-fuck myself in an attempt to sully all five of my digits, but that seems a bit unwieldy, and also absolves fifty percent of my available hands from their fate, which might finally give my teeth ideas about destruction of my available nails. But I simply cannot – please don't say that what I really mean is "will not" – because it really doesn't make that much fucking difference in the scheme of things, now, does it. I can't give up that pleasure – yes, it is a pleasure to me – a pleasure that actually, like the tongue/tooth example, fills an empty place in my soul. Stop shaking your heads! I know it's pathetic. I also know what you're thinking: I will never ever ever actually ever grow up into maturity where I might become "stable" and into a state that sloughs off its temporariness until I stop this one habit. You think I've never thought about this before? But I probably won't – or maybe I will. Or maybe that's not it at all. Maybe my fatal imperfections are just so basic that I will never be able to see them. I know where this is heading, you know: A deficit of L-O-V-E. That's it, isn't it. There's no way I can trace the route down that particular rabbit hole, but if you insist. Okay, okay. I turned my back on love. Satisfied? I can't remember their names, obviously, but there was that one guy who fucked me so silly that people at the baths thought I was actually dying in that deluxe full-sized room up there on the third floor. This guy must have had money because he sprang for that big room with the majorly huge bed instead of one of the dingy little single rooms that always smell a little like a mixture of bleach and shit. But getting back to the sex, Jesus fucking Jesus motherfucking Christ. I will never forget that. Afterward he wrote me a little note on an oversized business card, but with no hint of what his vocation or business was written on it. All it was was a small card of off-white cardstock – with little dark speckles here and there on it – a style I've since learned certainly costs more than plain white and which has earned for itself a perch on one of the many shelves of "elevated taste" – and he'd written his first name – which I've forgotten – and the words "I want more – MUCH more!" (his emphasis and exclamation mark – not mine) – and his phone number and address, which was somewhere down in the California desert – which, at that time in my life seemed a bit too exotic, like I didn't know at that tender time in my life that the California desert was a haven for homosexuals to accrete, as well as the notion that anybody'd travel longer than eight blocks to get laid seemed just so stupid. But here's the thing: When he got dressed in his street clothes, he put on these Lawrence of Arabia really loose-fitting harem clothes, like gossamer white bed sheets that had been made into casual clothes, and I guess my mind took the decision-making duty right away from me when I saw those clothes, because I just couldn't fit that "look" into my life in any way at all at that time because in this respect I'm like every other human being on earth: Every person I've been intimate with is automatically cast into predictive roles of future acceptance or non-acceptance, and I remember after watching him pull on these silly looking pants thinking how uncomfortable I would be on subsequent Christmases with my family – WTF – or how weird I would be treated by *his* family who probably lived in a deluxe yurt near some desert oasis, and all the gifts I'd receive from them would be harem clothes.

Or it might have been this guy named David – I'm saying "David" but it – yeah, I think that's it. He was an artist, but so incredibly handsome – like an actor in a beer commercial or maybe one for fast cars. And he *loved* me. I mean he was hopelessly in love with me. But screw it. Sex with David or whatever was a chore because he had this really long but seriously skinny dick – and he fancied himself a total top and he'd get my clothes off and he'd start thrusting and shit, but Jesus, it hurt, but not in a good way. Not. At. All! David had a little white house way out in the Calabasas Hills, and it was like

120

immaculate, like not one bit of dust in it at all. And the "art" he made was what he called reverse glass painting, which he explained was exactly how the images on pinball machines were created, where the artist had to paint the last brushstroke first, which, according to David, was a process that was right up there along with painting the *Mona Lisa*, and turned out to be a subject that I'd never once until that time in my life had ever thought about – I'm not a pinball kind of guy. And right away the process seemed a little – boring – but I was polite because he was so handsome and I felt obliged to imagine a life lived with David and his skinny dick. And he treated me chivalrously, which was another detail that bugged me. Always made me feel like I should be dressed in a ballroom gown or something where I'd start to feel "conspicuous." Probably starting to get warm, so if I were a betting man, I'd say this all stemmed from motherfucking David with the skinny dick. Because that whole conspicuous thing kind of makes so much more sense right about now. So my problems just might be totally connected to this David guy, but who really knows? There's no way to literally go back and examine anything without maybe being hypnotized, but that's cause-and-effect for you, I guess. But don't get me wrong. I really did used to be happy. I must have been, right? No one on earth has been fucked up from day one, right?

I know times change and everything, but back then – back when I was young and didn't have so many problems – shit never used to be so serious before all this "awareness" shit that's around today. We didn't do drugs really, except smoke pot and take acid now and again. And we weren't such fucking victims either. God! I'd blow my brains out in the next couple of seconds if I turned into one of those bitter old queens who complains about everything all the time – actually I wonder if any of those guys is actually able to see the progression of their reasons for being as they cross the boundary from minor annoyance to constant victimhood. Either that or maybe turning into one of those leather clad relics who hangs around leather bars every afternoon and you'll maybe be slumming one day and will have ducked inside into the darkness for a while, and one of these old dudes will inevitably walk over and start to take liberties, verbally speaking, and just out of the blue say something like, "Everything you think's happening isn't," which might literally ruin your afternoon because you're not ready for it, and you've got your own fucking problems out the ass but you're just here for a little respite from the world – but that's what it's designed to do is totally knock you off balance so that maybe, in a moment of weakness or indecision that might be brought up by just about anything in your life, like maybe your dog's sick or your thoughts have been consumed by increasing mention of "the gay cancer" on the news every night, and you might be feeling a little sick, or any fucking thing actually – or you're maybe questioning everything you've ever done or thought, and this old relic's indecision meter is pretty finely tuned and he offers a weird form of intimacy available to "special" people like you that will end up being some kind of succor or something, that he's tried to get you to believe would be stupid to turn down – or maybe they'll be some kindly old grandpa who kind of places a huge amount of stock on "happiness" and he just says, "Why don't you smile," which, when it's happened to me, I just feel like stabbing whoever's said it. And I'm not saying that victimhood hasn't been a "good" thing in the long run. I mean, if we just kept our mouths shut, AIDS would probably have killed us all off. It was just different back a long time ago. For a really good time, gay guys used to dress like nuns and drink wine and smoke not very strong pot. Period. I've heard the stories. It was so – good natured – so innocent. I used to love to hear their stories from when these old queens were young. They'd get dressed up in drag, but not like the kind of drag that's popular now, like all those TV shows and all that LGBTQ stuff, where the women they're trying to imitate are like Godzilla with big tits and metallic hair, but it was something so different, and I would love to have seen it. It was all about cunning and being clever – kind of like reading a book instead of thinking that you can entertain somebody with something "novel" from the realm of mass media. I remember once a few years back on this Sunday afternoon I asked one of my neighbors – this old guy who lived downstairs from me – I asked him if he wanted to go see a Spielberg movie – I think it was one of those fake dinosaur ones with the major special effects. And he seemed ambivalent at the suggestion and so I right away said, "Oh, come on! Go with me! It would be good entertainment!" And I remember his eyebrows raised for a second and he said in this way I'll never forget:

"Do you think that *I* want to be entertained?" like the whole concept of "entertainment" was just so vulgar to him, but he smiled anyway and I couldn't really tell if he was being serious or not, but I thought his answer was really fucking cool. Anyway, drag used to not be such a big deal. The whole idea was to dress up like a plain Jane kind of woman, one who held down an office job who typed really really well and answered phones and wore "sensible" shoes and not much makeup where making a spectacle of yourself just wasn't done. This one old queen told me that he used to get dressed up to resemble one of these plain Janes, and he was so good at it, no one – even at a gay get-together, would be able to tell if he was a guy or just some run-of-the-mill lesbian. The getup he described was a powder blue turtleneck fluffy kind of sweater with a modest crucifix hanging on the outside, unstylish glasses, of course, and a gray medium-length wool skirt – or maybe a pantsuit – and sensible shoes. He said he knew he'd nailed it if he got hit on by a lesbian instead of some seriously fucked up straight guy with tons of issues. And he said he'd never ever ever give away anything to anybody – he'd keep it all "inside" – like the joke was just that precious – until he got back home or back someplace with his buddies, and then they'd fucking let loose and howl and cackle like crazy about how much fun it was blending in to the female wallpaper. Anyway, I can just imagine seeing all these bearded guys wearing habits crossing some busy street in Silver Lake – right out in the daylight. They smoked cigars and they didn't give a shit, but they weren't all fucked up with some kind of a "mission" like everybody is today. They were just having a good time. And I knew some of these old queens and they treated me like I was something. And we'd head over to Mr. Brott's apartment over on Lucile – he and his roommate had a terrace, but nobody really liked his roommate much – his name was Lee something or other – and I can only remember that his astrological sign was Pisces, which seemed really really appropriate for such a wishy-washy type of person. He worried *all* the time! *"Oh, I think we've smoked enough pot"* or *"Oh, I think we've had enough coffee"* or *"Oh, that wine isn't free, you know. I think we've had enough."* What a fucking loser Lee was. Brott pronounced his name like it was spelled "Brote," but it actually should have sounded like "brought." And we smoked pot together and Bill Brott – we called him Mr. Brott on

Sundays for some reason – well, Bill would wait until we got seriously drunk and totally stupid on this shitty weed, and he had this dorky jeweled box about the size of the Kleenex box. And he'd dig it out of some closet and carry it out on the terrace along with his Mason jar-full of cheap red wine – there was this big black button right in the middle of the box. And he'd explain that we were gonna drink "lemon-aid" but he pronounced it "lemon-ahhhd," kind of like that white girl in *Auntie Mame* – the one with the ping-pong balls and that unlikely pubescent relationship with a man who should have known better because he was portrayed as somebody with solid character who should have had more discernment in his girlfriend picker than he obviously had – and blow up rich peoples' houses while we lounged on the terrace there getting unconscious and sloppy. And Mr. Brott – Bill – would give me this box and tell me to look off in the distance toward the Hollywood sign where all these mansions are in the hills. And he'd tell me to pick out one of these houses that I'd like to blow up with explosives, which would happen if I pushed the button. And then I'd settle on some big old house that had all these white turrets and outside walls that were tall and topped with orange roof tiles and was supposed to look like a Moorish castle or some shit, and push the button down and Boom! The house would be blown to smithereens. Not really, you know. The explosions weren't real, but it sure was fun imagining you have all that power – it had a real kind of Roman emperor feeling to it. And everybody would choose a house to blow up and push the button and everybody would yell "Boom!" and we'd lounge around for a while and laugh and cackle like hell and drink "lemon-ahd" and it was just so much fun because it was on this great terrace with all these guys who used to dress like nuns and go out in the sunshine. I met Bill – Mr. Brott – when I just got to LA from Arkansas. I had this cool part-time job in an antique store and Bill used to come in and buy stuff there. I guess saying "antique store" isn't exactly accurate – it was more of a thrift store with old shit. And Bill picked out a chair made of bamboo that he wanted to look at, and he always used to tell me this story – he'd say I was really enthusiastic about this style of chair and he did an impression of what I said way back then: "Ah luv rattan" – but the "rattan" I said sounded more like "ra-tay-yan." I loved Mr. Brott. He's gone now though. Don't you understand? Please tell me you understand. Wait a minute though. If you're sitting there judging me because I'm gay, if that's the basis for your attitude, then hold the horses for quick second. If it turns out that that's the case, then all I have for you is one more giant *Fuck You*, because come on. You really can't be serious, right? This is motherfucking Hollywood and you're judging me because you "suspect" I might suck cock? You just wish I'd suck your cock, right? Keep on wishing, asshole!

###

Jimmy moves across the boulevard in spurts and starts, expending way more energy than necessary, much like his less-than-tranquil sleeping style. He looks like a cross between a '70s V-8 Crown Vic who's forgotten that it's been banished to spend its golden years while beating itself to death in a demolition derby with other similarly aged vehicles, and a groveling apologist pleading to be left alone. He heads west toward Martel and that huge modern apartment complex where The Geisha has lived for the past six months or so. Jimmy tries to resist thinking poorly about the Geisha because somewhere deep down in his memory he remembers a time when he was a more generous man, when he took with a grain of salt humanity's imperfections as simply the necessary parts of some great beautiful tapestry. At one time Jimmy may have tried to stuff his dislike of the Geisha into a manageable little bindle and perhaps decided to visit another vendor instead of the one he's become used to – to add perspective to unpleasant tasks. But that's the thing about habits. The Geisha's an asshole. It has something to do with putting on airs. Actually, hardly anybody likes him. He's a low-level dealer who behaves the way he thinks drug dealers should act – meaning that he holds court and wastes everybody's time, even though it's pretty obvious that this behavior is born from choice instead of necessity: *my dealer wasted my time, so I will waste everybody else's time.* But as luck would have it, once the doorbell is pushed, Jimmy's given speedy admittance and, once inside the building's lobby, he takes the elevator up to the Sixth Floor, where he prepares himself to endure the usual duties The Geisha burdens on him after he's slammed a half-gram of free meth into his veins. The Geisha's price for a "free" shot of speed is the substantial duty of trying to administer a shot to The Geisha himself, a task peppered with pitfalls that would test the endurance of bona fide surgeons and saints, much less the enfeebled abilities and attention span of Jimmy S. As they are in obese people, The Geisha's veins are practically invisible. But The Geisha's not overweight. His veins are diminished because he's diminished – physically speaking. He appears almost gossamer, and it wouldn't be surprising if he jumped out of his sixth floor window and just floated away with the breeze, which in Hollywood, actually smells a little bit like bad milk most of the time. But that's just the obvious physical challenge of the task. Anticipation of an impending rush will cause most dope fiends who are hard to hit to insist that whoever is doing the hitting to just keep jabbing, which always results in a bloody mess. And dope fiends being original examples of low self-worth, will often offer their arms as sacrifices to the cause. The existential challenge lies in the post-shot neighborhood, because 1) after receiving a shot, The Geisha gets completely Tandaleo of the Jungle, murmuring and drooling over whatever piece of meat is nearby (Jimmy), and performing a come-fuck-me Dance of Salome; and 2) once the dope hits him, The Geisha shits his panties.

CHAPTER FOURTEEN

Sometimes in *deluxe* recovery facilities a cloud of adversity arrives and casts its shadow over everything and everyone, which can cause even the most powerful and esteemed former addicts to rely on their current undrugged, undesperate, unsullied circumstances to shape their reaction to new stimuli that will result in them forgetting their most basic mission, which is to keep drugs out of the facility. George P. was such a dark cloud – not really a cloud, but more like a plague, so powerful and cunning – and charming was his performance that even MaryAnn and Ben, the husband and wife *there's-no-doubt-that-we're-hope-to-die-no-hope-drug-addicts* founders and current directors of the facility, fell for his act. George P. was a black man who'd arrived at Cri-Life from Corcoran Prison, where he was serving a twenty-five-year sentence for killing somebody, which should have been a pretty strong hint that one might consider taking him with a grain of salt before accepting the truth of his presenting persona, which was figuratively and literally a tap-dancing Uncle Tom complete with profound stammer and downcast eyes. Every morning George would shuffle into the tech office and charm all who witnessed him: *"Ca-ca-ca-caaaan I jus' get sum soap?"* The staff, both permanent and temporary, almost ninety-nine percent of whom were white, a fact not lost on George, who'd perfectly predicted the reaction to not only the unassuming, humble nature of his query, but the entirely self-effacing manner with which it was delivered: "Of course, you can have some soap, George! Here, take several."

George always refused the offer of extra soap: *"N-n-n-no thank ye, ma'am/sah – one'll be fine wid me. Th-th-thank ye kindly though,"* the reaction to which, after the prescribed number of repetitions, was universal: "Poor George. George is so – sweet – and clean! Poor George!"

George was neither sweet nor deserving of sympathy – and the "clean" referred to only described the kind made possible by the use of soap and water. Shortly after arriving at the facility, George devised a method to have large quantities of heroin dropped at various points around the perimeter of Cri-Life, something that kept him and dozens of the most sinister clients behind its walls completely gowed for months, almost all of whom confessed, after the scheme and its attendant contraband were discovered, that George was no stammering tap dancer. During the investigation that followed George's Shit Storm, he was described by those who partook with him as a cold-hearted monk with perfect diction and a laser focus of intent. He was no more an Uncle Tom than was William Rhenquist. Even before he'd climbed off the prison bus that bore him from the verdant north of the state all the way to the parched wasteland of North Hollywood, George quickly banished the welcoming arms of Cri-Life, its staff and its promise of a meaningful life unimpaired by heroin or cocaine or any other substance directly and without reservation to the realm of "quaint." He was being true to the promise he'd made to himself decades earlier: If he somehow exited the walls of Corcoran Prison not in a pine box, he was going to get high. Period.

In the annals of detailed record keeping in the state mandated hourly, daily and weekly journals describing life at Cri-Life, there has never been such an upheaval as was precipitated by the appearance of George P. It was, to put it bluntly, the kind of mess that all institutions, be they small like Cri-Life or bigger like the Catholic Church, inevitably experience, no matter how redundant their safeguards seem to be.

So after the initial excision of obviously "guilty" residents (which included George P., obviously), an Investigation began in earnest, and fairly quickly grew and took shape during marathon meetings held between Ben and MaryAnn, and many of the most trusted hierarchy of administrators and CDWs, a messy schedule-destroying condition that most of these administrators and CDWs accepted as a necessary step to getting the facility back on track, but that some, including Rick, equated with dying and going to Heaven. Possibly because he'd studied law, but probably because he retained the status of being one of the all-time biggest solid gold assholes who'd ever walked the earth, staff meetings to Rick came as close to scoring a bull's eye in terms of hitting his sweet spot as anything else in existence. To be fair, society is better off because of meetings. Meetings are the essential test tubes of compromise and consensus when it comes to shaping policy about everything from how to address pandemics to cobbling together train schedules to devising signage with the most appropriate language with which to shame healthy youths into relinquishing their seats so that the elderly and disabled on public transportation might have a spot to sit on. And to the spiritually centered kind of person with generous hearts, intellects and souls, meetings are necessarily tedious affairs that are to be endured. But not for Rick. He thrived in meetings, not only offering his thoughts at every opportunity, he even relieved Cathy P., the *de facto* taker of minutes from meeting to meeting, a duty that Rick took responsibility for due to some early fatherly advice which laid out in no uncertain terms the importance of being able to shape the record of official proceedings, legal or not.

"*Become friends with the court stenographer, son. Buy him/her gifts – fuck 'em if you'd like, but remember this: it's the record that's important, not what people think they said,*" advice that actually turns out to be pretty much true for a number of reasons: 1) No matter how much this or that interlocutor might object to inaccuracies in the official transcript of proceedings, it's the record that's considered sacrosanct. The note taker is the last word. 2) Laziness. The process available to actually challenge the accuracy of a legal transcript is so onerous that it becomes counterproductive, actually having the ability to cut into the barrister's allotted time to collect his/her sacred fees. To underscore his commitment to record keeping, Rick's father actually, sometime in the 1960s when personalized license plates were introduced in California, had learned from a friendly court stenographer, whom he'd met during one of his first criminal trials – and had actually impregnated after one of many alcohol-fueled post-trial get-togethers when he'd followed this stenographer into the ladies' room of Trader Vic's, the traditional watering ground/party palace for much of the west side's legal community, how to spell certain words with their little shorthand machines. He'd had the letters *tpubg u* emblazoned onto his de Ville's license plates, groupings of letters that the

Department of Motor Vehicles only a decade later learned meant Fuck You when unpacked into plain old English words. Being a pretty sharp cookie, Rick's father had discerned the fact that his number one son, Rick, had, probably from birth, but certainly in his formative years, displayed traits that suggested he was prone to taking it up the ass, and being true to his impossibly progressive ideals, had encouraged Rick, after he'd graduated from the law school at Loyola University, to have *tpubg phe* imprinted on his license plates, the shorthand equivalent of Fuck Me.

It was during one of the many meetings at Cri-Life that Rick, in a surprising flash of creativity, suggested that maybe – just *maybe* – the arrival of George P. was actually a blessing, a statement that guaranteed him unwavering attention from everybody in the room. The biggest hurdle facing most recovery facilities in California is fiscal. There is never enough money, something that, according to Rick, could be solved easily enough with the help of George P. It's been stated that recovery houses aren't democracies. True enough. But one thing that they are is fair, at least when rendered in very broad strokes, something that Rick saw as only a minor impediment to his plan of identifying undesirable residents, then kicking them out after linking them, whether it was true or not, with George P.'s boondoggle.

And Rick, being himself a pretty sharp cookie, had offered his own unsolicited rejoinder to the as yet realized objections: Complete with raised palm with which to ward off dissents, and signifying *please allow me to continue,* Rick offered the overused aphorism that's often dredged up by lazy debaters to address injustice: *"Life just isn't fair sometimes – but we must consider the greater good – no?"* Rick thought that ending this declarative statement with a negative query imbued it with a certain academic gravitas, and had actually, the first time he heard it just before earning his bachelor's degree in Physical Therapy, given him goose bumps when the Intro to Human Kinesiology instructor had offered the proposition: *"A good shoulders routine is just the same as poetry, no?"* Put simply, Rick proposed using the catastrophe brought on by George P.'s introduction of heroin into the facility as the springboard that could be used for kicking out every state-funded-dope-fiend-who-at-least-presents-as-someone-who-wants-a-better-life, which necessarily included 100 percent of the gang bangers, about ninety-five percent of the crackheads, and about eighty-five percent of the AIDS/HIV cohort, which would leave veritable acres of unused, pristine and empty beds languishing for a warm and necessarily flush-with-money private-pay client, a state of recovery house grace that the administrators who ran facilities in Malibu had honed to perfection over the decades.

There were, of course, the expected amount of disapproving *harrumphs* from most of the meeting attendees, along with a peppering of *sforzandi* achieved by table slapping and a generous amount of plain old *fuck yous* to express disbelief and outrage.

"*That would fundamentally change the face of Cri-Life!*"

"*Ridiculous suggestion!*"

"*How dare you!*" – expressions that only fueled Rick's arguments.

Disapproval was met, point by point, with seemingly well-thought out evidence – complete with charts and graphs that Rick had fashioned over the two weeks that had passed since George was kicked out. In the process of making his case to the assembled hierarchy of Cri-Life officials, Rick wanted to be perceived as the grownup in the room, generously listening to and weighing dissenting arguments which flowed from the mouths of folks like Janice E., and all her "hokey-pokey" world view, to many of the heavily tattooed ex-cons of a certain age, whose societal aspirations, due to the completely successful brainwashing born from decades of institutional living and which took shape simply because they didn't know any better, were necessarily foreshortened into a guttural chorus of phlegm-heavy exhales, to Ben and MaryAnn, who seemed more befuddled than argumentative. Rick waited for a lull in the anti-Rick cacophony to pepper his loftily-perched positions with a generous amount of buttery impatience: "*You will perhaps allow me to say…I speak now with sincerity…You will forgive me for expressing myself with, shall I say, frankness,*" a style of speech that pretty much disarmed most of those present, whose rhetorical templates had been modeled over the years, after the silver tongues of Jerry Springer, Glenn Beck and various prison employees.

Grudgingly, Rick's position won out, and he, of course, volunteered to become Cri-Life's tip of the spear in its wholesale restructuring, and it was a duty that Rick turned out to be quite good at. But more than embodying merely the tip of the spear, Rick assumed the responsibility of being the spear's entire shaft as well. He convinced everyone in attendance that his plan could only be successful if it were left to him to painstakingly if need be question each of the Cri-Life residents one by one. As mentioned earlier, Rick had a remarkable smile – not because of the way some people's smiles reflect the benevolence of their souls, or the way they might invite intimacy. Rick's smile was remarkable because of its overt artifice. He bleached his teeth several times a week, which rendered the sight of them while he was fashioning a grin as something more akin to a blazing Klieg light rather than as a reflection of his humanity. Even if he'd wanted to intimidate the residents by donning the costume of a medieval inquisitor, complete with miter, orb and staff, the simple act of smiling struck fear into their hearts. Also, the brightness of his teeth was set off and accentuated not by his clothes, which were simply Levis or khakis along with various button-down shirts, but by his impressive musculature, the *Yeah, I know I'm ripped* kind; and skin tone, which he maintained at a dark latte hue. Rick preferred to search out the objects of his inquiries rather than having them simply report to his office, a strategy that he believed imbued his mission with a certain alleatoric quality, and was something that he thought gave him a tactical advantage because of its unpredictability. With clipboard in hand, he could be seen standing just outside the thick glass double doors that led to the facility's smoking/hanging around patio, and scanning his list of targets and comparing them to whomever was in his line of sight, then stopping to ruminate for a few moments on the best way to present. Just as Bernard Gui, in the fourteenth century had compiled a handbook for inquisitors to study when searching out, questioning and ultimately exposing heretics to Roman Catholic dogma, Rick employed a similar tactic, albeit one a bit more improvised, but no less magisterial. Upon his initial approach to a subject, Rick became merciless and aggressive, but nevertheless retained an overtly-constructed warmth, something he believed would put his trembling targets more at ease. *"Hi, Audrey – very nice outfit you're wearing. Would you mind if I asked you a few questions? Would you mind very much if we could sit at the other end of the track – under the tree maybe for some shade?"* (broad smile) *"We'll have more privacy over there. After you, please."*

Even armed with the knowledge that most of the at-risk residents he intended to elicit tacit – or even not so tacit confessions from, were lightweights in terms of their rhetorical readiness with which to meet an interrogation – because – well, it's obvious: dope fiends are often the first ones to admit that they're the dregs of society with just about zero value compared to the hardworking broodmares and broodmasters of the world, whose worth can usually be measured by the size of their debt for the upkeep of said broods. Dope fiends are quick to admit to lying, which, in the scheme of things, are mere pebbles of societal transgressions compared to the boulders of bad behavior they'd prefer to keep mum about because the less that's really known about this shit, the better, right? Rick nevertheless questioned his targets in a meticulously baroque manner that turned out to prove the validity of Parkinson's Law: *The Job Expands to Fill the Time Allotted To Do It.*

There was no explicit timetable for Rick's plan. It was just assumed that he'd tackle the task with his usual efficiency, which, to the administrators meant alacrity, but to Rick meant thoroughness. Rick, unbeknownst to his Cri-Life masters, allocated himself huge swaths of time to interrogate the residents whom he wanted to give the heave-ho to. It became common practice that his questioning of one resident could last for multiple days, which, in Rick's mind not only guaranteed him steady and rewarding employment, but also scratched a heretofore unscratchable itch somewhere deep in his soul.

One happy (at least for Rick) byproduct of this bloated approach, was that it was rendered a process that was not unlike watching paint dry, or grass grow – or listening to the music of Philip Glass, or even that John Cage piece called ORGAN^2/ASLP that had, to this point, been performed continuously for thirty-plus years in an abandoned cathedral in Germany somewhere, and was written to last 639 years, which rendered it the world's only piece of music that necessarily placed appreciation of anything but mere fractions of its whole outside the capabilities of humankind – or any earthly life form outside the genus of redwood trees – or there's that thousand-year-old olive tree, but that's probably not really true because religion – because each change in the music – no matter how small – took place every six years: Rick's questioning mechanism proceeded so slowly that it took the residents it was aimed at too long to discern its true intent. Once that line was crossed, however – once the correlation between being approached and questioned by Rick and the pursuant dismissal from the facility was discerned, wholesale, albeit whispered, panic set in among the most sinister and marginal of Cri-Life residents. When Rick approached you, you were a goner.

Because of Cri-Life's naïve population – at least in terms of meeting Rick's Inquisition, prayer and luck – or prayers for luck – became the favored means by which residents hoped to be spared, because they were mostly painfully aware that even though Cri-Life wasn't perfect, and was often difficult, it at least gave them three squares and a daily shower and a clean bed, not to mention a chance to imagine a life not locked up, or a life that could come to its conclusion by natural, meaning unstabbed/unshot hopefully peaceful means. It became a common practice for the most hardened criminals to band together in their respective rooms late at night into earnest circles where they would pray for deliverance from Rick's attention. But it was the Hispanic residents – the ones who put on Spread most nights – who carried this fate-laden heavenly solicitation process to its ultimate form. What these tattooed gang-bangers lacked in real world sophistication was indemnified with a generous reliance on superstition, handed down, probably, by this or that *abuela* from the old country south of the border. Shortly after Rick's scheme was deduced by them, they began attaching talismans made up of collections of their pubic hair and toenails to the doorjambs of their rooms, objects with storied magical qualities which they hoped would help steer Rick away from seeing them as objects of his inquiries, much as Obi-Wan Kenobi used *The Force* to steer the scrutiny of various Imperial Storm Troopers from the likes of the lovable and adorable droids, R2D2 and C3PO.

###

Leading this practice, though, were the females of the house who, rather than bundling tiny clumps of their hair or nails and attaching them to their rooms' entrances, a strategy that the girls dismissed as being impoverished, provincial, and actually kind of quaint when compared to the magical powers of the Goddesses who ruled the earth in millennia past, *les filles hispaniques et leur amies blanches et noires* smeared spots of menstrual blood onto their doorjambs, a practice that imbued the ethos of the female floors with a certain feminine mystery so thick that not only the homosexual male staff members, but most of the overtly hetero ones too, began to secretly fear a necessary trip to a female floor, a task that came to be referred to as a dreaded journey to The Fallopian Jungle.

While the original Inquisitions of medieval Europe (and seventeenth century Massachusetts) relied, for the most part, on convincing suspected heretics to implicate their friends, families and neighbors in service of keeping their own asses a safe distance from the gallows or the fires, Rick, because of Cri-Life's really tiny (in comparison) population, was able to completely disregard (for the most part) any similar strategy. He didn't need snitches to achieve his goals. He knew whom he wanted to get rid of. But because of pesky state regulations designed to trace cause and effect – and ultimate indemnification from the ubiquitous lawsuits that have rendered California a society that more closely resembles one from the island of Japan where citizens are maniacally protected from every imagined obstacle to complete safety: If the Grand Canyon were somehow located in Japan rather than Arizona, it would make perfect sense that the entire canyon's perimeter would be – due to an unquestioned penchant to protect sightseers – lined with probably several thousand state-paid – all wearing freshly pressed blue skirts and white gloves – "safety personnel" to serve as a smiling and impossibly polite barrier and who would hold hands because of the fear that people just might jump off the edge if left to their own devices in order to protect themselves from gravity and free will, Rick was bound to elicit connections, be they real or imagined, between George P. and those whose next stop was Victory Boulevard. Rick's lengthy questioning amounted to nothing more than an elaborate pantomime. Even though there were fewer than a dozen residents who actually got high with George, Rick was easily able to get residents to implicate their best friends and acquaintances, usually with promises of preferred treatment (which never really materialized): "*If you tell me who you*

135

know for a fact helped George get his drugs into the facility, things will go easier for you."

As in the aforementioned Spanish Q&A, the Cri-Life pogroms had virtually the same effect, as premature, meaning before brains were completely washed and cured, ejection from the program, and actually equaled a modern-day version of *Auto-de-Fe,* which landed residents of the program out into the unprotected ether of society, where they were about as inconspicuous as a suspected Jew being burned at the stake before crowds of blood-thirsty Catholics, and ultimately proved to be just as lethal, since the preferred destination for most of the de-housed Cri-Life population amounted to anyplace with a baggie and a spoon, and resulted in either a mercifully quick overdose, or being reported to the authorities who quickly dispensed the prolonged torture of being returned to confinement in the state prison system.

Several residents and staff members who were kicked out of the facility and the surrounding circumstances:

1. Shoshanna. The decision to give Shoshanna the boot came before George's heroin scheme blew up. It was deduced that she'd violated the non-com rule, even though no firsthand evidence was ever presented. During high level meetings of the pre George P. debacle where various residents were evaluated for either retention or kicked-outedness, Rick suggested that no one really knew Shoshanna nor her intentions regarding faithfully following the House rules nor her post Cri-Life intentions as they pertained to following the funnel back into society, especially whether or not she really wanted to stop using drugs, if not for the rest of her life, then for the State-prescribed length of five years, a codified interval that spelled "success" in terms of recovery, and which added to the viability quotient of the facility, which was used in determining whether or not to award large chunks of tax-payer cash that kept the Cri-Life wheels turning from one fiscal year to the next. Rick posited – although he never admitted to having any evidence – that Shoshanna had freely and with malice aforethought communicated with Rogarth during one of their many visits to the AIDS Clinic. It was, after all, her overt enthusiasm at volunteering at every opportunity that sealed her fate, said

enthusiasm having caused tongues to wag, gazes to narrow and
judgments to sprout, basically taking on the patina of *too-good-to-be-
true*, which has just about no place in the taxonomy of Cri-Life levels
of recovery. After only a bit of necessary head shaking and teeth
sucking, the staff voted to send Shoshanna packing, which meant, of
course, a speedy ride directly to state prison, which was a shame
really because there is little in life that's as magnificent as driving
down Victory Boulevard at ten in the morning or two in the afternoon
and seeing one of the hardcore Cri-Life *bitches* on foot in front of the
facility, whether she'd been kicked out or not, and making her way
down the sidewalk – when it seems pretty obvious that being out in
public during daylight hours is not only a novelty for most of them,
they don't even try to fit in. They're as aware as anyone else on earth
that their mere presence in the course of normal affairs amounts to a
giant fuck you, whether it's the way their hair falls down their backs,
their overt sexuality, their collections of tattoos and/or track marks.
It's certainly all of the these, but more than anything it's the gait – the
tempo and rhythm of how they walk – it's like maybe seeing a grand
cruise ship that, for some reason, had found itself out of the water,
and who instinctively knows that trying to fit in would be futile, so
onward it moves, making its way back to water or nighttime or
whatever. Even someone so misshapen as Shoshanna would be a
wonder to behold if she'd been given a chance to make her way down
the boulevard free from the protective Cri-Life *umbra*.

2. El Ocho. Even though his drug tests came up clean, El Ocho
(referred to during staff meetings as Bernardo Guzman) was kicked
out because he was neither silent nor effusive during his treatment.
Cri-Life funding: the State of California's Department of
Corrections...about 1/6th of the money paid by private insurance or
family fortunes. El Ocho had been able to turn down the inevitable
offer of Ryan White funding, which was even less than that from the
State...obvious reasons. Connection to George P.: close, because that's
how Rick wanted it to be.

3. Eric P. Part of the HIV/AIDS cohort; Ryan White funding.
Connection to George P., minimal. Arrived at Cri-Life because of his

status of Failed Alumnus of LA's only 100 percent homosexual recovery facility: Van Nuys Recovery House. To Eric's credit, he stood up to the VNRH's full-time and storied Mistress, Bethie Blatt, who runs the place with a muscular infallibility, an iron fist inside a titanium glove. Unlike Rick's *ad hoc* system of rooting out undesirables from Cri-Life's ranks, Ms. Blatt was – and has always been within anyone's memory – a full-time Seer, Confessor and Inquisitor. She alone decides whether any given addict can stay or leave, a position of power she jealously and maniacally protects. Eric did last for a respectable 2.5 months inside the walls of the House of Van Nuys, and while there he dutifully snitched on himself and others and immediately rang the "horny bell" whenever he (or she, depending on the available plumbing) began to have amorous thoughts about another resident of the House, two of the most basic components of an unimpeded, meaning Blatt-less stay in the facility. Ms. Blatt dismissed him from residency after stating that she was simply unconvinced as to the purity of Eric's intentions, or the quality of his honesty. Fortunately for Eric, Cri-Life decided to take him in with a minimum of being "wait listed," which kept Eric's probation for drug trafficking from being violated, one of the stipulations of which was uninterrupted treatment at a recovery house…"uninterrupted" being a fairly fluid term when interpreted by overworked prosecutors in courtrooms in the City of Angels. Unfortunately, though, he arrived at Cri-Life while burdened with a healthy dose of VNRH ethos/vernacular, two examples of which go something like this: Claiming transitive verbal properties for the word "incest," a detail that grew from living for a period of time within a certain tribe which placed uncommon value on the act of confession, whether it was true or not, and which it was believed added salience to the cause side of the cause-effect equation when asked the question: *Why do you think you want to use drugs in the first place*, the answer to which could be anything under the sun, but somehow clutched on to the reprehensible act of incest, a noun, which was allowed – and even encouraged behind VNRH walls – to traverse the linguistic gulf dividing parts of speech so that it came to be accepted as a verb: *I was incested*, a revealed detail that almost always elicited generous amounts of downcast gazes, shaking heads and sympathy, and which absolved the speaker of any responsibility at all for the state of his/her crumbling life. The second unfortunate vestige of VN influence was claiming verb-hood (another verb – what's the deal with verbs anyway?) for the first part of the noun *transistor* when describing the graduation process from the Van Nuys Recovery House itself, the non-word *transist,* which, one can only imagine, was an idea hatched by some Jurassic pervert who'd come to reason in a certain decade – at least someone who should have known better, given the quality of education as it pertained to grammar instruction in California public schools in the 1960s and '70s, so he/she was probably not listening in class or was challenged somehow, which is fine and dandy, but really, stay on your side of the street, please, and stop making up words because even though *transist* seems like it would, on a good day, suggest movement or matriculation or graduation or whatever, from one thing to another, because it *almost* rhymes with transit, but it's just the base of the word transistor, which was a word ubiquitous in the 1960s because they were the life's blood of tiny radios (*I got a transistor radio for Christmas!*) and great-grandfatherly computers the size of box cars, and is defined as an electronic component to be used to either switch the path of electrical power or amplify it. *Transist* was an invented word pressed into service to describe the process of completing the Van Nuys Recovery House program: *I'm transisting on Friday. Please come, I'd love to see you there!* a ceremony festooned with freshly printed Certificates of Completion (all 8.5 X 11 for some weird reason) and are dripping with momentous moments and grateful gratitude, and was actually, whether it was designed for this or not, a vehicle with which to beg for a measly number of square feet of some sober older homo's couch where the freshly minted, sober graduate might park his out-of-work ass for a few weeks while he sorts things out. At least, as a verb, *transist* was stripped of its transitive properties, which somehow endowed it with less vitality than maybe a word like murder when used as a verb. Whether it was explicitly stated or not, these two VNRH details had a tough time finding any bedrock of acceptance or even tolerance at Cri-Life, because – who knows why – but they nevertheless made Rick's job just that much easier.

4. Garrett. Hunky, corn-fed (wholesome looking) one-legged guy in his mid-twenties who'd earned the title of *resident tech* shortly after he reached the ninety-day mark of his stay at Cri-Life. State of California prison funding. Unlimited energy and enthusiasm; unflagging adherence to the House rules and their spirit. If you met Garrett on the street, he could easily be pegged as a Mormon missionary, albeit one with a prosthetic leg, a handicap he bore with unusual good cheer. Garrett has often inspired profound disappointment in many of the homos of a certain age inside the facility because his genuine altruism for All People of All Stripes has been mistaken for an urge for intimacy of the cock-sucking variety. Once it became apparent that his appetites were Jesus fueled instead of queer curious, most of the homos (at least the ones with enfeebled imaginations) gathered their balls and stomped off the playground. Some of the more savvy fags, though, nevertheless still tried to engage Garrett, as they had a sneaking suspicion that he'd dangled his organic non-plastic toes into the steamy waters of Lake Homo at one or several times in his young life. His plastic leg hardly slows him down at all, as, on a daily basis – oftentimes multiple times per day, he bounds up and down the stairs leading to floors two and three at the facility where he is tasked to deliver important messages to the residents or procure the presence of someone or other so that Cri-Life justice can be meted out. One remarkable bit of dissonance that defines Garrett is the way his presenting demeanor contrasts so severely with the story of how he'd lost his leg. It was in a dope deal. Not the kind of dope deal that most of us are familiar with, the kind that consist of amounts of money less than $100 and dope amounts in increments measured in grams or maybe a bit more. The kind of dope deal that got Garrett's leg blown off with the blast of a sawed-off shot gun was the kind measured in hundreds of thousands of dollars and multiple pounds of product. And it doesn't matter who shot whom and for what – suffice it to say that Garrett found himself on the wrong end of the barrel, and has, since that afternoon in the back of that van, been scarred for life.

5. Balthozar Allendé. Flush with cash from an impossibly privileged family headed by male progenitors who've been a staple in

the United States Diplomatic Corps for generations. Balthozar presents as asexual, not because he's not sexy or anything – he's simply uninterested – in anything. Nothing – at least nothing within the walls of the facility – arouses his curiosity. He seems to meet life with an overly complete repertoire of yawns. When pressed to participate, it becomes clear that, being a bona fide heroin addict, he's escaped the effects of the legal transgressions that any addict, regardless of funding sources, at several times now and then, take part in, due to dope sickness, which is the ultimate motivator, not only because his family has been there to bail him out, but also blind fucking luck. He's been arrested numerous times, but never convicted of anything more serious than trespassing, which seems to be the "go-to" infraction of choice for offenders who can afford private counsel, no matter what the underlying offense really is – short of maybe murder or something like that, though. And he's polite. His stay at Cri-Life represents the tiniest of draws on the petty cash drawer of his family's substantial coffers. One way that describes Balthozar's demeanor consists of imagining him the director of gospel choir at a Black church, and who in his progress through endless days of potent ennui, instead of rehearsing and performing a blindingly rousing rendition of the gospel staple "O Happy Day!," which is the musical embodiment of the ultimate acceptance of God's joyful deliverance and redemption from the costs of sin, Balthozar would have chosen as part of the choir's repertoire an anthem titled "O Acceptable Day...," (elipses included so that there can be no question as to his intentions, which are meandering and pointless at best.) More than anyone at Cri-Life, Balthozar Allendé represents the greatest threat to the primacy of Rick, at least as it might erode his pretention to royalty. Balthozar's probably rimmed (and been rimmed) by more legitimate kings and queens than Rick can imagine, which renders Rick's Queen Jadwida story pretty flaccid in comparison, so in Rick's mind he had to go.

CHAPTER FIFTEEN

I'm on the spot. Korn just sips his Coke – and I've already said that I'm hungry – *really* hungry. The plump counter guy has generously given us each a set of white plastic utensils, which I don't really want to use because, in my long experience with plastic knives and forks, this particular class of knife, fork and spoon is just too flimsy to get the job done. Tines break off and the knives simply bend into unusable forms and the spoons seem to be only good for scooping up dandelions. I want to pick the whole burrito up and eat it in maybe three or four bites tops, but these burritos are of the "wet" variety. Picking them up would be as messy as scarfing down ribs at some barbeque joint. But with seemingly unlimited patience, Korn's just sipping his Coke and sawing away at a tiny portion of the delectable stuffed flour tortilla. I'm jealous, and I'm also salivating.

"We gotta use what we have to work with," Korn says without looking up.

"Yeah, so what," I say.

He looks right at me: "These knives and forks," he says. "As nice a place as Antonio's is, they don't really furnish stainless steel utensils – they give us these. Takes patience."

"Impossible," I say. "Look."

And I give Korn a demonstration by diving in and trying to saw through the stuffed flour tortilla, which leaves both the knife and fork a mangled mess.

"Your expectations aren't realistic," he says.

"My expectations are just to eat," I say. "I'm really fucking hungry."

"See this?" he says, as he licks the red sauce off his white knife and holds it up.

"Yeah, I know. It's pathetic. Adding serrated edges to something

142

so flimsy is ridiculous."

"Nah," he says. "It's all about your expectations. The whole point of serration is to multiply one cutting edge into many, which makes total sense, even if the material it's made of is flimsy, like this plastic knife, or hard like a Samurai sword, or your dad's steak knives way back at home. Remember them? The purpose of each one of the serrations is to reduce the point of contact between the cutting instrument and what's being cut, kind of like the difference between punching a hole through a piece of leather with an ice pick or a baseball bat. Think of it that way. Each of these little serrations makes it possible to literally rend a piece of flesh – or a flour tortilla – or a sirloin steak – but with movements that are commensurate with the size of the cutting edge and its strength. And being for the moment in California, we should all – whether it's conscious or not – be aware that this state itself has a cutting edge – and I'm only talking geography here – and not some vague notion called Hollywood, unless you think spending hundreds of millions of dollars on dropping cars from airplanes has anything to do with telling stories – then fine. Hollywood is fucking avant garde in that case, and each brand new sequel that's shit out with a numeral from II to VI tacked on the ass end of its title is hoped will be just the cookie cutter cutting edge that will finally tear the jugular vein of discrimination from the public so that every last drop of integrity is encouraged to leak out into the cultural storm drains of the world. I'm talking about the mountains. California's serrated cutting edge is called the Sierras, those jagged mountains that bisect the length of the state. Because of the Sierras, Planet Earth is tearing the shit out of space using California's serrated cutting edge – or maybe not – but just for argument's sake, maybe at least pretend that earth's prow, as it hurtles through space, is California. Or on a micro level, maybe California is the template for the design of sharks' teeth, which all have these repetitious bumps, these – he puts a little swirly English on the word's emphasis: "Serr" – and rolls the R: – "r-r-r-ations." He continues:

"Sharks' teeth are serrated for the same reason. They make sharks more efficient when they eat – kind of like what I'm doing and what you'd like to do. Forgive me, Bert. I get carried away sometimes. But back to California for a minute. Do you think it's just a happy coincidence that 'Sierra' and 'serrated,' as words, look similar? What came first? The idea or the mountains? But then again, there's that road of privilege in Santa Barbara, Alameda Padre Serra – or APS as it's known to the locals. Onomastically speaking, Junipero Padre Serra was the cutting edge of the Catholic Church here in the Golden State – a double edged serrated cutting instrument that cut out the souls of California's Chumash population so that the Roman Catholic Church might have a place to fester here. So think of these little flimsy white knives as maybe the original cutting instruments used to cut out raw unadulterated faith. It must have taken immeasurable patience. Know your strength and know your enemy. And the indigenous population who were successfully converted from a vague faith in the benevolence of Nature into a fearful belief in the Holy Trinity? They all became flimsy copies of the good father's repeated cutting edges – thousands of them, cutting and sawing and tearing the soul from this state – not to mention the American perpetuation of the Spanish and Roman knives in Europe, even here in the City of Angels where there was literally, in a preferred form of *Auto-de-fe*, one Jew burned at the stake for being a heretic."

I want to tell Korn that he's just jacking off, mentally speaking. But I don't. I force myself to become comfortable in my discomfort – at least less uncomfortable, because I'm starting to panic and I want, more than anything, to avoid any kind of existential crisis, something I've never been good at. I hope Korn won't notice that my breathing has quickened and that I've begun to surreptitiously scan the place for an escape route.

"Lighten up," he says, then turns away from me.

"Excuse me!" Korn yells to the plump counter guy. "Can you bring more knives and forks for my friend Bert, please."

"Sure thing," the guy answers to Korn.

And he dutifully scurries over and deposits a brand new set of plastic utensils before me.

Korn gently grasps the guy's arm.

"And please," Korn says – there's an unusual kindness in his voice as he speaks – "is there any way you could put on some different music…please?"

Amazingly, at that exact moment, the oom-pah-pah mariachi music comes to an abrupt halt, which produces quizzical looks from all of us, including the counter guy.

"That's was weird," the WOOF guy says, and he heads to his post inside the kitchen to check on the problem.

After a few moments, he returns to our table: "Looks like our iPod took a dump."

Korn says he didn't bring any music with him – and neither did I.

The counter guy asks if it's okay if we listen to the radio, which can be hooked in to the PA system pretty easily, and Korn says sure, to go for it.

The counter guy has hooked the radio into the PA system and scanned a few stations on the FM band before landing on a preferred station, and the resultant sprint through several of the news stations and heavy metal offerings kind of affords the same kind of experience as maybe a philharmonic orchestra tuning up before the maestro takes the podium, but not as thrilling – or hopeful. With finality, the search through radio signals ends on LA's classical music station, and there's that announcer – do they call classical music announcers disk jockeys? – whose voice makes you want to scream to the radio: blow your fucking nose, dude!, he comes on and lazily, with an effete phlegm-ridden mien, although also with a rising melisma of pronunciation and intonation, kind of lets the word *"Mazurkas"* slither from his lips.

CHAPTER SIXTEEN

Taciturn: A person of reserved or uncommunicative speech.

"G-d, if *only!*" thinks Moishe Silverstein, beads of sweat growing on his forehead and his forearm, as he furiously masturbates while he sits on the toilet and entertains a memory of his mother describing his father's personality. Moishe forces himself to concentrate, mentally squeezing images of his tyrannical judgmental father, arms crossed, mouthing the word "sinner" while shaking his head in disgust, out of his thoughts. "That's like calling Hitler impolite!" and "I'll bet Hitler's parents let him at least have his own thoughts once in a while." Moishe bears down. He beats his cock faster, hoping that his fury will steer his lustful thoughts toward Sarah Blattman instead of Ryan Gossling.

It's Friday night, the Sabbath. Moishe lives with his parents at 2044 South Kenmore Ave., right across the street from Korn's house. His mother's name is Ruth and his father's name is Chayim. His father is a storekeeper who sells Kosher meats in the Pico/Robertson area – Chayim's (Star of David) Kosher Meats – and has twice in Moishe's lifetime been caught representing to his customers that certain of the most popular meats in his store were Kosher when, in fact, they were cuts of meat he'd purchased on sale – *from Mexicans* – and were as far from Kosher as Vienna sausages swimming in a bowl of ice-cold Half & Half and cornflakes. There wasn't a rabbi around these cuts of meat for miles. Moishe is, if anything, trying to be a dutiful son. He knows better than to construct chains of cause-and-effect psychological elements about why his father is such a son of a bitch, but sometimes he can't help it. It's obvious, he thinks. His father is trying to atone for his Kosher meat wrongdoing by judging his son's thoughts, like he's able to report to G-d that – oh, G-d – Moishe stops beating off and gulps hard – that *I like boys,* as if he'd been caught making out with Ryan – or any boy, which he never has because he knows it's sinful and he believes the stories about G-d's punishment for being a fagela. Moishe's cock goes limp. "Fuck you, G-d. Fuck you, dad. You satisfied?" He pulls his pants up and looks at himself in the mirror while he washes his hands, the peyes on either side of his face stuck in place by perspiration. Moishe pulls them free and shakes his head, then goes into his bedroom, grabs his fedora and heads toward the front door of his house. Before he even gets his hand on the doorknob, his mother yells: "Moishe, where are you going at this hour? It's almost six o'clock!" He says he's going to his friend Dav's house to study for shule. He's pretty sure his mom won't object to this trip, as Dav just lives up the street so Moishe won't have to ride his bicycle to anywhere that might be farther away, which would be a sin on the Sabbath. But instead of turning right toward Dav's house, Moishe turns left and walks down Kenmore toward Olympic. He figures he's already sinned enough for a couple of weeks with all the masturbation, so he plans on taking the bus over to Vermont, which, even though he won't technically be driving the bus, he's pretty sure that just riding it is still a sin. "Fuck it," he thinks.

CHAPTER SEVENTEEN

Rogarth steps over a dog turd that's lying horizontally across the sidewalk, and he turns to warn Gallagher about it. "Watch out for that," he says. Gallagher sidesteps it and says, "Thanks," but realizes that his thanks is a form of gratitude that's broader than appreciation for his friend's level of awareness re: the turd. Gallagher wonders about the reasons that he and Rogarth are friends, not discounting the notion that their camaraderie may actually be based on the fact that neither he nor Rogarth listens to music when they're out in the world, a detail that's, here and there at times, piqued his interest, sociologically speaking, because it *is* a little bit interesting – really. Several times he's been tempted to acquire an iPod or similar device so that he can add music to his experience of the world – like just about everybody else in existence does. But there's something that restrains him. He hasn't really thought about this in much detail yet, but wonders about why the idea of listening to music in public makes him uneasy. If either he or Rogarth had earphones in his ears blasting this or that hand-picked music while walking down this sidewalk, it would be adding a soundtrack to what they're seeing in real time: El Pollo Loco, Quiznos, homeless guys, dope fiends, businessmen, thieves, thousands of cars and thousands of people, birds – all the "shit" that makes up being outdoors, everything would be mediated somehow with this soundtrack. So what? So what if adding music to someone's experiences of the world around him can be made more – more agreeable; less objectionable? That's the thing, he thinks. Would the world be a better place with the addition of a soundtrack? Would the world be made a little less ugly?

Or would the music itself be elevated as it busily attends to its genetic role of creating tonal tapestries and/or puzzles which, due to its performative, time-based existence, can trick the listener into believing that music exists in the spectator's service and functions to only spice up a pretty dull piece of scenery? Or just – what?

But Gallagher's pretty sure that if Rogarth had been listening to his favorite music during their walk, that the turd he was warned about would become just another facet of endorsement making up his worldview; part of some kind of inert tableau that was musically tailored to reaffirm his own sensibilities, like it might reduce the already meager level of curiosity he already possesses. After all, it's not like somebody else would have chosen which music was blaring into his aural canal, which, if actually the case, would have at least allowed for a more robust sense of wonder instead of just plain old validation – one more time – of one's tastes and appetites. Regardless of who chose the music, though, listening to it probably wouldn't include a warning to avoid the turd, so Gallagher thinks he'd probably, right about now, be cussing out loud while scraping shit off his shoe.

Gallagher doesn't mention his thoughts re: the potential of experiencing a musically accompanied turd, but goes right on talking about the teacher of his English class, volunteering that regardless of whether his English teacher is a philistine or not, he suspects he's going to get a B or maybe an A- for the course, as he's turned in almost all the assignments – at least the important ones; that he doesn't really think the SRs – Summary Responses – two-page reflections based on either a) a short story or journalistic article from a newspaper, or b) one of the chapters in one of the books in the class – are that important so he's only turned in a few of those.

Rogarth says something like "awesome," then Gallagher asks Rogarth how his math class is going, and Rogarth says they should change the subject; math isn't his best subject, then suggests that they should head over to Starbucks to get a couple of iced lattes before they buy their burritos for dinner.

It's pretty much the same routine every Wednesday for these guys. They make a quick right turn and cross Vermont Avenue, and even before they reach the other side, they're checking out a few of the most pious of Alcoholics Anonymous acolytes who've begun to congregate on the smoking patio at Starbucks for the purpose of a) assassinating the characters of many of their sober brethren/sistren or

b) earnestly discussing the concepts of Service to the less fortunate and/or God's will for themselves and others and/or trading anecdotes that prove the existence of a loving god and/or reading from handwritten tomes of dredged up memories that outline various transgressions to fellow human beings, better known as *reading your inventory of sins to your sponsor.* This latter category is the easiest to identify because of the ubiquity of paper notebooks and multiple writing implements, and the limiting of no more than two people per table, which, in less homosexually tinged arenas, these couples would be pretty much same-sexed because of the unwritten albeit pretty durable rule that dictates that prospective sponsees should choose their sobriety mentors from pools of identically gendered human beings, while the more progressive homosexually-leaning addicts have banished such rules to the cultural trash bin because there can be little sexual deviousness between sexes, so women sponsor men and vice versa. There's also a pretty potent Force Field of Explicit and Serious Intimacy surrounding these binary spaces, so people governed by more casual considerations know instinctively to steer clear.

Rogarth and Gallagher, not unlike most human beings, at least in Western democracies, enjoy believing that their lives are and always have been governed by their conscious choices, when in reality it's pure simple, stupid chance that's herded almost all of them to their current destinations. The only Starbucks table that's available, which is adjacent to one where Gordon B. (eighteen months sober) and Gordon's best friend William (not Bill; seven months sober) sit, so Rogarth and Gallagher, each clutching his clear plastic throwaway cup that drips with icy condensation, seat themselves with the potent authority of free men. They are comfortable for the moment in their situation of being roommates in a single second-floor apartment after leaving the sober-living house they'd moved into, at slightly staggered times, after leaving the regimented existence of Cri-Life. And they're in Hollywood, which somehow confirms for them that they're in the correct place in the scheme of things – assuming, of course, that there actually *is* a scheme of things, which is usually a fertile subject for discussion around the tables at this Starbucks, but as luck would have it, neither Rogarth nor Gallagher have to broach any subject at all because their attention is drawn to the adjacent table where Gordon and William are enjoying a moment of sober euphoria that's not unlike a weird hit of acid or having swallowed a couple of powerful bennies that has them enthusiastically, and with complete abandon, sharing their thoughts with each other about literally what the fuck ever enters their brains – a breathless recitation of each element that makes up an, if not completely empty, but certainly uncritical head while living in an unimpaired life. It almost sounds like a competition – an example of perfected improvisation where the rules of discourse can never be deliberately or even accidentally to disagree, but to enthusiastically concur with his partner and add another detail, an *and/also* strategy that changes the landscape and subject of any conversation into unrecognizable albeit felicitous forms from whence it had begun. It's completely unclear what Gordon and William had started talking about, but for the moment it's a certain movie they'd seen that afternoon. And it doesn't matter what movie it was, because Gordon and William are like most Americans, so their criticism of any movie can be boiled down to just how creepy, realistic, scary, sad, funny, suspenseful the *story* is and, of course, the special effects. It's grounds for a revolution, really, because movies have such potential. To show the truth. To show the cannibalistic monsters who eat movie producers and potential for breakfast. Movie makers are just human – and rarely heroic, so they usually compromise with the money people. And they're usually bright and retain vestiges of creativity, and many of them have learned to bury a movie's almost unlimited potential to tell a story by repurposing the artistic axiom, *Real creativity can only really occur when it's constrained within a strict framework of rules* into a form that relies on a kind of passive osmosis that has made possible the way most Hollywood films can be described, which is often a version of this:

Heroine (pretty; comfortable; sexy) happily bakes Bundt cake for family.

Heroine marks time by the progress of Bundt cake (which is almost done).

Heroine resists urge to call husband (handsome; manly;

powerful; naturally drawn to Bundt cake as the embodiment of heaven) and looks out window of kitchen – sees agreeable suburban street/neighbors, who, it's understood, have healthy Bundt cake appetites.

Heroine removes Bundt cake from oven at exactly the same moment that the phone rings.

Heroine has suffered a minor finger burn from Bundt cake pan, and she sticks finger into mouth before answering the phone, which creates a morsel of levity because it's hard to talk with a finger in your mouth.

It's heroine's husband calling to report that he's been held up at work (he's a Bundt cake patent attorney or a designer of Bundt cake ovens, or possibly ex-CIA analyst of Bundt cakes ([foreign Bundt cake division] because Hollywood), when it's revealed he's calling from a mid-priced hotel room that's seedy yet clean because it's pretty obvious that residual stains have literally been sanded away, leaving a pathetic, well-worn patina here and there for which the film's Art Department went over budget by about $125,000 just to get "the look" just right because the director has lost the ability to discern the difference between necessary and unnecessary detail, and where the husband's spent the afternoon fucking a super-delicious *non*-Bundt cake baker/eater with a questionable moral center.

Heroine reports that the kids aren't home from the mall yet (the mall represents interstitial space between Bundt cake/no Bundt cake). It's learned, due to acting chops, that husband isn't a dick; he's just flawed – like anybody actually because who could resist fucking a woman that fucking beautiful – he loves his family – and probably has an enormous capacity for atonement (which includes his refusal to partake in proffered Bundt cake from friendly characters who aren't aware of the depth of his flaws, so they're left with open-mouthed acceptance/astonishment) that will be expected in about 75 minutes of movie time.

Amid fussing with the pristine Bundt cake – ok, maybe just a piece is missing – the heroine pours herself a glass of red wine and sips it while at the same time she flogs herself (flaws) .

Authorities are called re: missing kids (stale Bundt cake in generic detective office in seedy section of Downtown – crumbs *everywhere*). But the point is that these detectives are "good" guys because Bundt cake.

Attention drawn to several really bad bad guys who've kidnapped the kids and are vaguely torturing them because kids (withholding Bundt cake from them). We know the depth of these guys' rottenness because they smoke cigarettes, they have morsels of non Bundt cake food in their teeth, along with the fact that they couldn't care less about good Bundt cake, which is demonstrated by them eating beef sandwiches instead of Bundt cake.

Mish-mash of shit involving good intentions (Bundt cake), flawed husband (morally questionable prostitute non-Bundt cake baker/eater) and bad guys (cigarettes/dirty teeth/kids) and forlorn wife (Bundt cake in the trash).

Husband *almost* gets his kids harmed severely because he's flawed – he's strayed from the potent-yet-passive innocent allure of Bundt cake.

Heroine indignant and pissed (fresh Bundt cake in the trash – *again* – signifying the literal end of Western civilization – anyway, it's really fucking awful).

Husband rises above his flaws to rescue kids, but wife/heroine – due to blind self will – is imprisoned by same bad guys because she's pissed (succumbing to influence of flaws), illustrated by her having thoughtlessly and recklessly bought a cheap generic Bundt cake from a 7-Eleven (also a flaw).

Kids/flawed husband-dad outsmart bad guys, illustrated by them secretly and earnestly eating a hastily concocted Bundt cake that's been made using "found" ingredients, and then hatching a plan.

Flaws of main characters rendered flaccid and inert by triumph of human spirit embodied by billboards touting A-1 first class Bundt cakes. The Great Lesson of Returning to Genuine Appreciation of Bundt Cake has been learned and *internalized*.

Freshly baked Bundt cake enjoyed by all.

Of course the foregoing is a slightly reduced version of exactly what it was Gordon and William were discussing – and the film could possibly have been one involving real-looking dinosaurs or international thieves instead of run-of-the-mill bad guys, but the Bundt cake remains (or something signifying Bundt cake because Bundt cake equals all things good and clean and pretty and white, which this last thing Hollywood producers would *never* admit to [the "white" thing] because they're these really powerful people who rarely make pernicious decisions because they vote Democratic and donate $$ to third-world countries and they make a point of being indignant at all things that might be interpreted as racist, even though a casual survey of their early children's cartoons, which are, of course, suitable for the entire family, will reveal that they've rendered all the minor characters offered to provide comic relief because they're inept, as well as the truly bad bad guys in their stories as either black or dark), but it's not their fault really, it's just the "cowboy" white hat/black hat thing, and barring earnest examination/study by people who know a thing or two about culture who might be able to offer helpful suggestions, the cartoons and later work remain monuments to ignorance, not to mention that that kind of study is time consuming and probably really really expensive, so fucking sue me, you nit-picking liberal assholes, the Bundt cake stays because it's a signifier that's – hopefully – as basic as Bambi-generated pathos, rooting for the morally superior underdog or plain old overcoming lust for your neighbor's mom or dad, and what do you think? I'm doing this for the fun of it?

The point is that William and Gordon really enjoyed the film.

(Note: Both William and Gordon listen to downloaded music on portable devices – just saying)

Once the film has been sufficiently discussed, William (in his own quiet way) calls for calm at their table and he announces solemnly that he's begun working the Eighth Step of the Alcoholics Anonymous program, which is making a written list of all persons you've harmed during the time of your chemical impairment so that you can make amends to them. Gordon only nods in complete support, and William then says loudly enough to be overheard by most of the adjacent tables: "Of course I put myself at the *top* of the list!" where the *"top"* in the sentence is literally and musically at least an octave higher than the rest of the words in his proclamation. Most of those who've heard this remark take it as a matter of course. But some – mainly those people who've suffered multiple relapses and have had objectively a much harder time with this twelve-step thing than most – know that such a statement is not only technically wrong – the Eighth Step doesn't mention a word about making amends to yourself – they know it's also morally wrong; that the whole concept of making amends is a risk-laden adventure in character building: There are some people who've been shit on by impaired alcoholics/drug addicts, who, in spite of how well the recovering addict/alcoholic is doing at the moment, will never accept your fucking amends no matter how earnest you seem at the moment or how pure your intentions are. That's in the literature. But where's the risk when you make amends to yourself?

Hi self, I just want to say that I'm really really really sorry about stealing that $30,000 and forcing you to lose your business and get you like arrested and stuff, and that I'll never do that again and, if it's not too much trouble, do you think you could forgive me; and if you could signify/codify this forgiveness by giving me a pretty robust hug – a mirror hug even though it's me I'm talking to right now, right here in public. I'm not ashamed at all – come on, big fella! Bring it in here!

What are the chances that you're going to decline an offer of amends from yourself?

Oh, not so fast, self. You really fucked with me and you forced me to behave badly and reduced my standing as a human being with all those drugs, and I'm not as forgiving as some people, so fuck you.

So self-forgiveness remains as a marker of assiduous character building. Gallagher fixes his sight on the entrance to the burrito place across Vermont.

"Hey," he says. "Isn't that those two guys we just met?"

"Yeah, looks like it," Rogarth says.

"You wanna go over and see what's up?"

Rogarth's stomach does a somersault as a memory of a speed rush takes shape in his head.

"You think it's a good idea?" Gallagher says.

"Sure – let's go."

Gallagher says: "What if they ask us if we get high?"

CHAPTER EIGHTEEN

Jimmy S. has been successful. He's crossed The Geisha's finish line and, fortified once again with a healthy dose of meth coursing through his veins, he pushes the elevator's call button repeatedly, even knowing deep down that repetitions, at least in this case, probably have about zero effect at speeding the process. He jumps inside and rides to the street level, where he emerges into a world of glorious possibility. Governed at the moment by an expanse of time that's grown to dimensions beyond his comprehension, Jimmy points himself vaguely eastward in the direction of Korn's house. He's buoyed with thoughts of conquest once again – of discovering, exploiting and ultimately tearing into the sexual fantasies of some unassuming young man. With a practiced ease, different scenarios take shape in his imagination, each a category of a possible target: Cops? EMTs? Jihadists? He realizes, as the eastbound Sunset bus arrives, that he's begun to foam at the corners of his mouth, and silently orders himself to take it easy; that he'll have all night to find the perfect partner.

CHAPTER NINETEEN

I've settled into a pretty comfortable eating rhythm: carefully sawing the burrito, stabbing the morsel, and depositing it into my mouth. It's tedious and I'm not feeling exactly satisfied. The radio seems to have grown louder and the announcer guy with the overflowing sinuses on the loudspeakers inside Antonio's forces my attention. There's a certain level of difficulty in his voice. He digresses before he condescends to allow the music to commence:

"If I may, please permit me to offer my opinion about what may be the basis for so many problems in society: We've simply forgotten how to dance." And he gives an unsolicited little explanation of the *Mazurka* tinged, of course, with a diphthong-heavy sea of snot, and, it seems, way too much time on his hands. "The *Mazurka*," he says – he seems to have lost most of his enthusiasm, settling instead on a pretty comfortable bed of professorial languor – "is a Polish dance not unlike the minuet. It's written in 3/4 meter, but ideally" – and he stresses that word again – he's getting excited again – "*ideally,* it's performed *and* danced" – as if this emphasized conjunction "*and*" will pique everybody's attention and raise this discursive lecture into some higher realm.

"It's danced *and* performed at a meter that's somewhere in the middle between 3/4 and 2/4, so that the music *and* the dance literally hover over a magical space that's undefinable, but at the same time unmistakable. It's like drawing a secret breath where no one expects you to do anything at all except maybe defy gravity and fly away – or what's likely to be the case – hmmm, let's think of a pretty common example of interstitiality, like something that really has nothing to do with music or disease or physiology. Something like inter-species stuff. Batmen? No…too obvious. Wolf-boys, then. How about that? How might you expect a regular human boy to behave who'd been raised by wolves? There's a tried and true example that won't tax the imaginations of the listening public too much…and it's certainly not without precedent.

"Would this wolf-boy's behavior hover equally between the two forces: nature/nurture? Or would he resist expectations and favor wolf world or human world? Or would he take on characteristics no one could predict? Or would he just end up being a reflection of the dominant culture that's able to tell stories about wolf boys and growl here and there when offered a piece of meat instead of something else, like – oh, god, would he devolve into merely an expression of deficiency where an audience of humans would quietly cheer for his inborn capacity for human cleverness to take over and demand that something like knives and forks be invented where none existed before the present moment? Or would he be something else? What would 'something else' look like? Would it be hideous? I like to think so. I like to think this boy – we'll call him Dave – I like to think that Dave has become comfortable with emotional pain because the wolf leaders have certain expectations of other males in their pack, which almost always boils down to making a move on one or more of their females, but due to Dave's complete inability to experience coitus with the wolf bitches, because – well, suffice it to say they have insurmountable differences, which Dave tries to overcome, but he just can't. And this inability causes Dave to suffer substantial embarrassment and swaths of self-doubt.

"But Dave's also become comfortable with physical pain because his wolf parents/siblings are always chewing on his flesh, taking bites here and there, even when he sleeps, and this becomes so routine that Dave actually – because he's actually human with a ton more brain power than his wolf caretakers – starts to expect this feeling so he's learned to take bites off himself because he's from the Midwest originally and he possesses an almost superhuman capacity for accommodation even if he dislikes what's happening. He absolutely hates to disappoint – so he overcomes the pain and just munches away at himself believing that this is what's expected of him. And this habit grows to horrific dimensions until he can no longer bite off any meaningful parts anymore – he's already swallowed his hands and feet and limbs and his cock and balls (what a pity!), so the only thing left is his torso and head, which are out of reach because that's where his mouth resides and his neck only stretches so far, and even with unrelenting practice and concentration, Dave simply cannot overcome this physical constraint, so he eventually goes quite mad, due to not only the frustration of impossibility, but also to being defined by his peers and teachers as a disappointment, until he reaches old age, but he still, now and then, remembers to try to eat what's left of himself, but he can't.

"And after Dave finally dies, the wolves just think this is what all human boys must be like, but they nevertheless miss him quite a lot because they'd grown fond of the way he tasted, at least as an adolescent or even a young man because they're objectively so delicious – and let's face it: old guys are pretty much just gristle, fat and hair. Who in his right mind would hire a masseur to come over for a hundred bucks or so and strip naked if he was some old guy masseur who advertised alongside the youngsters? Yuck!"

The radio announcer takes a breather from his lecture here, but do we get music yet, just to maybe hear this magical musical phenomenon? No.

He continues: "But alas, the Mazurka – and not *just* the Mazurka" – he digresses again – "both the Mazurka *and* the *minuet* are hardly ever performed correctly, the Mazurka for the secret rhythmic place where it should reside, and the minuet because of the erosion by popular culture of definitions. I get the whole 'social relativism' thing and how essential that is for some things, like academia and 'cultural progress' – probably for Democracy itself – but it has a dark side" – And the guy's starting to get a little excited again, but this excitement only sounds like the phlegm in in throat is starting to boil a little: "But certain things should have meaning. So sue me, kick me off the air. But please, if you can't tell me that there's any difference between 'less' and 'fewer' or 'his/hers' and 'their,' then just shoot me. Banish me to Rigid Formalist World because apparently that's where I belong." He takes a breath and swallows what sounds like a lung-full of snot before he continues:

"Both the Mazurka *and* the minuet weren't what we've come to expect from watching Hollywood movies – they were, at the time of their popularity, more like an ancient form of dirty dancing – absolutely ribald and sexually suggestive. Sure the ladies wore yards and yards of satin over corseted middles and the men wore formal Rococo-style outfits. But at that time people weren't all that hygienic.

Picture the Prince's Ball where he courted Cinderella, but rather than a well-scrubbed room-full of prissy satin-clad ladies and gentlemen, they were all pretty much unbathed and filthy, and heavily scented, the perfume only having the ability to be effective at the very beginning of the ball. Their stink literally overpowered their layers of perfume and garments so that their high-classed ballroom, with magical twinkling candles and dignified string orchestra, smelled more like a skanky locker room with backed-up toilets than what we've come to imagine in minuet scenes rendered by Paramount Studios or whatever movie studio that exists in Hollywood. Try to picture this ball. The siren call of the Mazurka's seemingly unstable rhythm must have been irresistible to just about everybody in attendance. Within the framework of this 3/4 (or 2/4) beat, the people flung themselves at each other and groped and grinded and salivated like some primal mating dance that we've banished to 'lower realms' of animal life that promised forbidden debauchery – and all that perfume mixed in with all that stink and the ballroom's heat because obviously no A/C just aroused everyone all the more until sexual desire finally, at the end of the night, devolved into chicken fat-lubed fucking and some gag-heavy cock-sucking."

And at exactly the moment when I'm beginning to question whether what's coming out from the speakers is really a radio station at all, finally – *finally* the Mazurka starts and what he's said is true. I'm completely overtaken by the music's meter, which seems more than I'd bargained for at the moment. It's grabbed me and, it seems, Korn too. And we're transfixed with its strength – its tyranny, because it's grown irresistible. We've been grabbed by our collars and the dance is having its way with us, and just like the guy says, I'm trying to count: "ONE, two, three, ONE, two, three" – but there's a space that, once it's acknowledged, grows to engulf the entire meter until it transforms into something else – something *monstrous* – and I can tell that it's got both of us because we're both counting and holding our breath after the "two" and before the "three," and there we are, suspended – smack in the middle of this no-man's land between the two beats.

CHAPTER TWENTY

The bus Jimmy S. is on is approaching Kenmore Avenue, and Jimmy's experiencing a slight lull in his meth rush – the high has begun to show its finite side – so he has to make a couple of pretty substantial adjustments to his perception and expectations, so he jumps off the bus when a 7-Eleven store he's familiar with comes into view.

Before ducking inside, Jimmy quickly does a quick walk-around of the store's parking lot, especially over by the dumpsters, because there's sometimes a couple of crackheads over there who would probably be willing to drop their pants if they think Jimmy's got a quarter or fifty cents for them. But there's just some torn up heroin addict who's actually *kind of lounging – no shit, actually lounging* in all the spilled Coke and leaked mayonnaise and wilted lettuce and cellophane wrapping paper and pieces of crumbs of discarded Twinkies, and probably not-quite-dried puddles of piss and probably a few aromatic piles of human shit that's strewn around the dumpster, and he's like pushing forty or something and he's got cuts and bruises all over him and Jimmy's absolutely not going to waste his precious high on *him*, even though, Jimmy thinks, this guy was probably pretty good looking a few years back – his blond hair has a certain authentic robustness under all that filth and he's got the build of someone who's had, at one time or another, pretty good muscles – kind of like skateboarders and *fuck!* Jimmy *loves* those guys. And Jimmy wonders for a brief moment about maybe dragging this guy back to Korn's house and letting him take a shower, and probably feeding him whatever food's in the fridge. Korn's probably got some old clothes here or there that might fit him – and he knows he can throw this guy's raggedy, smelly old shoes right in the trash, because think about how grateful he would be with different kicks and socks! There's a tiny thrill taking shape in Jimmy's head shaped by the raunchiness quotient of diving into this guy's crotch that's probably been completely ignored and un-thought of by another human being for probably years at this point. *Ewww,* Jimmy says as he contemplates the unthinkable, the ecstasy of the inexorable descent into filth, and he becomes flushed with a slight fever of desire, and he *almost* takes a step toward this heroin guy, but he senses, off to his left side, a furtive presence that exudes youth and – what's most important to Jimmy – an *ethnicity* – a kind of youthful blur that's unmistakable – the looseness of black-and-white fabric – a style of dress he's become inured to while hanging at Korn's house, which up until a few months ago Jimmy'd only seen pictures of or seen on the news now and then – usually stories that have to do with Middle-East peace or lack of thereof – Jews – orthodox Jews with tzitzis and peyes and fedoras and prayer shawls – and naiveté of unbroken/unexamined faith – and most important: boyhood. This Jewish kid stops suddenly at the entrance and waits until the doors automatically open when some other guy hits the pressure plate of the switch. And this kid waits until the guy exits and the door completely closes again, then he rears back and jumps hard on the mat to trip the switch and open the door: *Dogma!* Jimmy doesn't mutter the word, but he instinctively recognizes the concept – the erosion of and rebellion out of youthful belief that's begging to be helped along and ultimately fouled and ruined – and his dick starts to get hard. In a flash he abandons his homeless heroin addict and darts toward the entrance of the store to check this kid out.

Jimmy enters the 7-Eleven with its unnaturally bright interior, which is pretty shocking to nighttime eyeballs, and like a big cat out on a desert savannah somewhere stalking a prospective dinner of water buffalo, Jimmy never lets this kid get out of his sight, even though he maintains a certain distance from him. This is what Jimmy's good at. He keeps his eye on this kid all the while making his way around the sticky buns and then the deodorant and now over by the bug spray. His confidence continues to grow as he watches this kid pay for a couple of sticks of beef jerky and a Slurpy – two things about which Jimmy can't know the significance. Both of these things – and thousands more – aren't kosher. But beyond simply being unkosher, they're literally *traif* – explicitly forbidden by God himself. This kid inches his way over to the magazine rack – *the left-hand side* of the magazine rack, which is the X-rated side. Perfect, Jimmy thinks.

This kid's all but in the bag. Jimmy isn't unaware of his own age, which he knows might turn off some younger guys, but he's got a secret weapon. He's been told for decades now – by just about every kind of person he can think of – that there's one phrase he's mastered that's pretty much irresistible every time he says it: *You wanna get high?* even though Jimmy doesn't think he'll have to resort to using it with this kid.

Jimmy makes his move. He quietly sidles up to the magazine rack and puts on a pretty convincing show of perusing a few magazines like *Car and Track,* bending and reaching now and again into the kid's personal space – a couple times he even squats and reaches over in front of the kid's knees so he can look up – just momentarily – and meet the kid's eyes, who are pretty much glued to images of either fully or partially naked people, because that's what he's there for.

"Sorry," Jimmy says a couple of times, or "excuse me." Jimmy knows that even one verbal response from the kid and he's a goner.

"That's cool," the kid says.

Bingo, Jimmy thinks, then: "I love that magazine."

"Huh?" The kid looks away from his magazine. He sounds breathless, a little scared.

Perfect.

"Your magazine. Very hot. I like that magazine you're reading."

"You want it?"

"No, no…I'm just saying…"

The kid shrinks from Jimmy.

"Hey, no worries, man. You okay?"

"Yeah, fine. What do you want?"

"Hey, take it easy. I'm just looking at a few magazines."

"I know who you are," the kid says.

"Wha…huh?"

"Kenmore Avenue. You live across the street from us – from me and my family."

Jimmy's expression widens into a smile: "No shit."

"Yeah," the kid says. "I see you – and your friends all the time."

Jimmy stands up straight and extends his hand: "I'm Jimmy."

"Moishe."

CHAPTER TWENTY-ONE

And I think about the musicians performing this *mazurka,* the courage it must have taken to plant a marker in a rhythmic place that can only really be guessed at. *That's not insignificant,* I think, as I imagine the bravery associated with discovery then exploring the unknown.

"Should we dance for a minute? Just to see?" I ask Korn.

So we start. Dancing.

It's probably not like legitimate mazurka dancing, because it's obvious: neither of us knows what dancing a Mazurka is supposed to look like. But Christ! It's easy as shit because who doesn't know how to count to fucking three? It's powerful; intoxicating. I forget about everything – *every fucking thing* – except the 1-2 – 3, 1-2 – 3 of this beat, until that's all there is, this beat and this space where we find ourselves between the "2" and the "3." There we are in Antonio's dancing like fools, and each time the "2" arrives, the chances we take are that much more daring as the gulf between the two beats increases; the space widens and deepens, inviting us to jump further. And both of us are laughing our heads off as we find ourselves in this unknown space – and it's not like rendered in a way that I can really describe it because I don't understand it except that I want more and more. And even the fat guy with WOOF printed on his shirt has begun to tap his foot to the music, and he's laughing his head off too. And the guy on the radio with the overflowing sinuses seems to know we're dancing, because I hear him urging us on: *That's right! Fuck 'em all! Don't forget to count! 1-2 – 3, 1-2 – 3! Keep it real! Fuck 'em ALL!* And the room and all that blue and white metal furniture starts to follow us and all the bullshit of everything starts to fall away: All those "shoulds" and "shouldn'ts" and the fucking HIV doctors who're so fond of portending doom with the phrase, *We expect* – like *"After a period of twenty years of being 'infected,' we (meaning the medical community) 'expect' symptoms to arise not only on the physical level, but the cognitive level,"* but we're still expected to be brave and civilized and polite and arrive to work a little early just to make a good impression, and buy donuts for everybody once a week. But I'm not pissed off at these expectations because I'm still breathing, and I'm thinking so what if it's hard? And for some reason I allow myself – for the first time in I don't know how long – to imagine traveling a road that isn't paved with injury and grievance – and I can hardly breathe the word: *entitlement.* Christ, I think – that's me. A fucking *entitled little bitch.* And I think of all those people who died of the virus, and not just AIDS, but of just plain old stupidity – all over the world, and I start to feel ashamed, but all I really give a damn about now is this beat, this 1, 2 – 3 and this dance – this *Marzuka.* And I can see myself dancing in the reflection of plate glass windows of Antonio's, and what's really cool is I see Korn too, and we're going back and forth looking at each other in real life, then looking at our reflections as we're fucking dancing our heads off. We're really dancing – I make a face at myself in my reflection. "Look at you, you fucking idiot!" I stick my tongue out. "Fuck you!" I yell at my own reflection, and I can't help it, but I'm really dancing like crazy. "Fuck you, fuck you, fuck you, fuck you," I yell, and I'm laughing my head off like a clown. And then Korn yells "Fuck you!" too, and we're both dancing and clowning like fools. And every time this space shows up between the "2" and the "3," we both hop a little bit higher, and on the way up we both inhale with the word "Fuck," and on the way down, into this space that seems to keep widening, we both yell "You," and the vowel part is elongated because the distance is elongated each time so it sounds like *Youuuuu.* And the fat guy with WOOF on his shirt has joined us. And I'm really kind of surprised at how robust his dance movements are, and he yells "Fuck you!" too. And he's hopping up at the "2" – way up, where he inhales on the way up just like Korn and me, and he's looking at his reflection in the glass too, and his *You* comes after the "2" but before the "3" – and there's all three of us yelling "Fuck" on the way up and "Youuuu" on the way down, and I try to force myself to experience this from a bit of a distance, and when I do this, the consonant "F" in Fuck kind of dissipates more and more until all I can really hear is *Uk Youuuuuu* repeating over and over coming from all three of us as we dance this Mazurka. And this makes me feel so good. And I feel so proud of this fat guy with WOOF on his shirt, like I get the feeling that this is the first time in his entire life that the phrase, FUCK YOU! has been uttered by him in a public place or around another human being, like up until this very moment, all the *Fuck Yous* from him had more than likely been muttered in private after yet another day of taunts and humiliation because he's always been fat and it's about fucking time. And I wait until this space between "2" and "3" opens up again, and I go over to him and I cup his face in my hands and just kind of goof on his beauty, and I yell "WOOF" at him as loud as I can, then I hug him really hard and I give him this huge wet kiss, and we both keep dancing, hopping up in the air and yelling *"Uk Youuuuu…"*

CHAPTER TWENTY-TWO

On their walk across the street, neither Gallagher or Rogarth says much; their thoughts are pretty much hovering around the question of how to react when these two guys ask them to get high.

Rogarth's tries to imagine the dialogue:

You guys party? You get high?

And just as Rogarth imagines his answer: "Well, no, but we *used* to get high," he remembers a similar time years ago when that answer produced nothing but searing, abject failure.

In a moment of Los Angeles pique, Rogarth had gone to the airport one weekend and taken a flight to San Francisco on a whim because he'd decided that San Francisco's *scene* was so much more authentic – more straight forward than what was happening in LA or Hollywood. So once he checked into his Folsom adjacent motel, he headed to one of SF's storied sex clubs/bars, one of those bars where *real* men hang out and that had straw strewn on the floor and smelled like beer and butt sex.

This all happened during a weekend when he'd just stopped smoking, so he'd only taken four cigarettes with him for the entire weekend, and he'd smoked the last of the smokes before leaving his motel.

So Rogarth wades into this bar – the testosterone hits him in waves, and he realizes he has to take a piss, a feeling that is pretty much thrilling for him because he knows about the bathrooms at San Francisco gay bars. It's a fucking party, very unlike LA heads, where there's a certain level of decorum, probably due to a particularly vigilant police force in the City of Angels. So Rogarth heads to the men's room and there's a line of guys waiting to go inside. And Rogarth is minding his own business and the line inches forward, and then the most handsome, sexiest, most self-assured guy in the entire universe takes his place in line just behind him. He's dressed in denim and is sporting a cowboy look, something that Rogarth suspects may not be an affect, because he has the look of authenticity, the kind of authenticity spawned by genuine humility that, if spoken, would produce the phrase, "Awe shucks, ma'am. I don't know 'bout that, but I thank ye kindly." Rogarth has been able to deduce the blinding degree of this guy's handsomeness simply by virtue of the vague quarter turns of his head that could have been explained away as simply curiosity about one's immediate surroundings – nothing to get upset about, so Rogarth has worked himself up into pretty much a frenzy, wanting to connect with this guy – on any level at all beyond, god forbid, *actually* getting him into bed – more than anything. But being restrained by shyness, or any number of legitimate psychological equivalences, he keeps silent. Finally, it's Rogarth's turn to enter the bathroom when the guy ahead of him exits, so he breathes deep and walks to the urinal, being absolutely careful to not appear too gay in his gait or walking style. And he pulls out his dick and only a couple of drops of piss come out because Rogarth is feeling so fucking nervous. And he wants more than anything to apologize to his Marlboro Man Adonis in line behind him, but all he does is look at the pathetic cock he's holding between a couple of fingers, and he gets the feeling that his cock is mocking him. *Mocked by my own cock!* because it's all shriveled up and might as well be dispensing grains of sand rather than piss at the moment. Actually, the only moisture escaping his entire body are a couple of beads of sweat that trickle their way down the back of his neck, causing Rogarth to worry about being judged for the prominent perspiration stains he imagines are growing on the back of his shirt. Time has slowed to an unacceptably slow pace, and finally – *finally* – Rogarth takes a chance and turns his head to see if his man's still there. And what he sees just makes matters worse: This best looking man in the universe, whose clothes fit just so, and – *every fucking thing about him* – Christ! The only thing missing from this guy's *look* is a piece of straw from the floor that he'd decided to suck on, that nonchalant *awe shucks ma'am, t'weren't nothin'!* kind of thing. And he's looking right at Rogarth and there's an unmistakable look of interest – *desire?* – there. Rogarth can't take his eyes of this guy because he's just so – just so goddamned handsome and this *can't be happening to me right now!* And as if the move were choreographed, this cowboy – all the while keeping his eyes pinned on Rogarth – reaches over to one of the bales of hay – *Shit! Rogarth thinks, THAT'S where the hay comes from! Bales of hay all stacked here and there for "atmosphere"! Why couldn't I have seen that before?* Anyway, this dreamy cowboy grabs a straw of hay and literally sticks it in his mouth while Rogarth's self-conscious paralysis has engulfed him entirely until he's feeling pretty much like a tower of salt. And just as Rogarth thinks he may as well just die right there in the bathroom of this gay bar, this cowboy speaks:

"Got a cigarette?"

Blood rushes back into Rogarth's face and he scrambles, as if his life depended on it, to offer an acceptable answer.

Why!? Why did he have to stop smoking on this weekend before coming to this bar? He's smoked his ration of weekend cigarettes – all four of them.

But Rogarth is, if anything, pretty much a straight up guy who knows deep down that lying at such an important and momentous moment wouldn't do, so he answers:

"No...*but I used to,*" an answer whose effect is like a curtain closing on the first act of a stage play of great potential, but has turned out to be a particularly boring technical exercise. The cowboy's smile disappears and without even a shrug or any acknowledgement at all, he heads off to greener pastures.

Rogarth slurps the remainder of his latte through his straw, then faces Gallagher and says: Let's just improvise – just see how we feel if they ask us if we wanna party.

And they both head off toward Antonio's.

CHAPTER TWENTY-THREE

You might think Jimmy'd be pretty much ecstatic by the way Moishe Silverstein is responding to his pretty much overtly homosexual overtures. He'd finally stood to face the young Jew, and had actually grabbed his own crotch with his free hand while he grasped Moishe's hand to shake. Moishe, it seemed to Jimmy, was at least ripe for the taking, if not actually beyond the *sell* date – overly ripe actually, a possibility that acted as a lullaby to his engorged cock, because this was *supposed* to be a conquest. He was supposed to *hunt,* to finagle his way through layers of refusal – and not just the normal garden variety straight-guy-dangling-his-toes-into-Lake-Buttsex refusal, but the much more delicious kind of refusal that tasted like sanctimony and had been baked in the oven of indignation and religious dogma. At best, he thought, this so called conquest was going to turn out to be mere pantomime because this kid was just too easy – there would be no conquest at all, much like having sex with a fake cop – just a step or two above mere theater – or what all those thousands of people experienced who'd traveled for miles and miles one August afternoon to go to Echo Park to see the Lotus Festival only to see one pathetic little lotus plant languishing at one end of the lake.

Jimmy's hard cock has wilted completely, but he's still holding Moishe's outstretched hand, and it's pretty obvious the kid is trembling. Jimmy knows he could torture this kid mercilessly by employing various delaying tactics – withholding cock from the needy – the cock deprived young Jew.

A question tries to escape from Moishe's mouth, but since all moisture has dried up in his mouth, all Jimmy hears is a breathy, anemic-sounding nondescript guttural phrase of sorts, but Jimmy knows exactly what he's trying to say:

Can we go to your house…now?

Jimmy releases the kid's hand and steps back – doesn't say a thing – just looks him up and down. Then with unmistakable resolve, Jimmy again takes a step toward Moishe, raises his arms and clamps his hands on both of the kid's shoulders and slowly pulls him close. He nuzzles the kid's neck with the kind of passion he didn't think he could muster anymore – the youthful brand of passion he'd almost forgotten about. And right there inside this 7-Eleven, under the bright unforgiving illumination of its fluorescent lighting, he bites Moishe's neck, then finds the kid's mouth, bites his lower lip, then kisses him deep and hard – he feels the kid's hard cock straining through his pants and against his thigh. And for a few moments they're lost in the passion of the moment, devouring each other's lips and tongues and necks and spit. Then with unmistakable resolve, Jimmy cups Moishe's cock and balls in one hand squeezes hard, which really shocks the hell out of this kid, but the kid endures the pain like a trooper – just the slightest whimper escaping his mouth. While still applying pressure to the kid's genitals, Jimmy blows his breath over the kid's neck, then moves to his ear and whispers:

"You go home now, Moishe. I'm not what you're looking for."

He pushes the kid away, and without looking back he leaves the store.

CHAPTER TWENTY-FOUR

Gallagher and Rogarth head inside the burrito place. It's quiet. No music; no kitchen sounds, just the vague sound of somebody murmuring to himself. The fat guy with WOOF printed on his shirt steps up to the counter:

"How you doin'? What can I get you?"

Gallagher says, "A chile verde burrito and a Coke," and Rogarth orders the same thing, except with a Diet Coke.

Rogarth peeks inside the patio area and doesn't see anybody. He asks the WOOF guy about the two guys who were here a few minutes ago.

"They're gone," the WOOF guy says.

"What do you mean they're gone?" Rogarth asks, a little annoyed. "Where'd they go?"

"I don't how else to say this: They're not here. They're gone – outta here – lost. Who knows. You want these to eat here or to go?"

Rogarth tells him that they'll take them out.

"You got it," the WOOF guy says.

View other Black Rose Writing titles at www.blackrosewriting.com/books and use promo code PRINT to receive a 20% discount when purchasing.

Made in the USA
San Bernardino, CA
15 September 2017